SO-AZZ-269

ALSO BY BETH PETERSON

Myrna Never Sleeps

No Turning Back

by **BETH PETERSON**

ATHENEUM BOOKS FOR YOUNG READERS

Atheneum Books for Young Readers
An imprint of Simon & Schuster Children's Publishing Division
1230 Avenue of the Americas
New York, New York 10020

Book design by Michael Nelson

The text of this book is set in New Baskerville.

First Edition
Printed in the United States of America
10 9 8 7 6 5 4 3 2 1

Library of Congress Cataloging-in-Publication Data
Peterson, Beth.
No turning back / by Beth Peterson.
p. cm.
Summary: When eleven-year-old Carol is killed in a hunting accident while
hiking, a mysterious wolverine, a wounded falcon, and a tiny bat help her
timid friend Dillon find his way back to civilization.
ISBN 0-689-31914-2
[1. Animals—Fiction. 2. Fear—Fiction.] I. Title.
PZ7.P44324No 1996
[Fic]—dc20
95-30857

For Nancy

No Turning Back

CHAPTER 1

With one earsplitting crack, everything had changed. Dillon couldn't remember pushing through the underbrush, but the scratches on his hands were proof that he had. Even now, he thought he could hear faint echoes of the shot rolling off over the hills. The sound of his own heart pounding in his head slowly subsided as he knelt at the foot of the hill beside the body of his friend.

Dillon never had many friends, especially good ones. He wasn't the kind of person to make friends easily, and his family had moved too often for friendships to last. Now that they'd come back to settle down in the house where his dad had grown up, he had acquired two good friends by his count.

One of them was whimpering now. Mary Jane, his

uncle's old hunting dog—his dog ever since his uncle passed away—was whining and sniffing Carol's face and hands.

Carol was his other good friend. She lay with her face turned away from him, at rest among faded wild-flowers and dry autumn grass. She had lain just like that, without moving, after tumbling and falling down the hill. Only her hair moved a little in the breeze. All the life had gone out of her when the shot had caught her and spun her around.

Dillon looked down at Carol and then glanced around at the wooded hillside, amazed at how quiet everything had become. He didn't know what to do. Surely, they would come. Surely, whoever had been shooting at the falcon would come and see the awful mistake they had made.

Mary Jane stopped whimpering and lay quietly, head on her paws, next to Carol. His two good friends had gotten along very well together. Of course, Carol got along well with almost everyone, thought Dillon, when she wasn't busy poring over her dad's bird books or hiking through the hills looking for hawks. She loved hawks.

In all of Dillon's nearly thirteen years, he'd never met such a bird enthusiast. In the spring, Carol had shown him where to find swallow and sparrow nests. She could spend hours watching a marsh hawk hunting low over a field or a redtail hawk circling high over-head. If she could have sprouted wings, Dillon thought, she would have been the happiest living thing on earth.

Suddenly Mary Jane sprang to her feet. Turning in the direction of the bushes behind Dillon, she bared her teeth. A low growl started up through her throat, becoming a deadly snarl as two figures came into view.

With one hand holding onto Mary Jane's collar, Dillon watched them approach. Two boys, both some years older than Dillon and each with a shotgun slung under one arm, stopped dead in their tracks when they caught sight of Carol. They stared, open-mouthed, in disbelief. Dillon knew, and they knew, that they shouldn't have been there with their guns a week short of hunting season. Even then, there was never a hunting season on falcons.

Dillon looked up at the boys from where he sat next to Carol. "She's, um," he began slowly, his voice barely audible. He cleared his throat and spoke again. "She's dead," he said as if surprised at his own words.

One of the boys swore, then turned to run back in the direction they'd come from. The other boy, looking stunned and confused, started walking toward Dillon. Mary Jane was still snarling and straining at her collar. The boy stopped short of the dog and seemed about to speak. Then, without a word, he too, turned and fled after the retreating figure of his friend.

"Wait. Come back," said Dillon, getting quickly to his feet. "You've got to help me. Come back," he called to the boys as they disappeared.

Dillon stood holding onto Mary Jane, wondering if he should go after them. He didn't want to leave Carol there alone, unprotected. If he waited, the boys might come back with help so he could get Carol home. At least, he hoped they'd come back.

They must have been the ones who did the shooting, he thought, then just strolled over to see what they'd hit. Why hadn't he yelled at them, they were as good as murderers, weren't they? And cowards too, running away like that. Maybe when they got home their parents would find out what had happened and somebody would come.

"It's okay, Mary Jane. We'll wait a bit," Dillon said as he sat down again. He put his arm around the old dog and scratched her neck, glad for her company. "Somebody's bound to come," he told her. Maybe a hiker or someone heard the shot, he told himself.

They sat quietly together in the warm afternoon sun. The sudden, unexpected shooting had left Dillon feeling dazed, as if all his thoughts and feelings had gone strangely quiet. He looked around, trying not to look at Carol. It just wasn't possible. It wasn't possible that she could be running and shouting one moment and be so very still the next. "Carol?" he whispered, hoping against hope. No answer came.

The whole world seemed to have become very quiet and still. Thin white clouds in the sky hung as motionless as if they'd been painted there. No insects buzzed, no birds called noisily to each other. The silent trees appeared taller as he looked up at them from his place on the ground. Like a dense wall, they rose up all around the clearing where he sat.

His grandmother had told him stories about these

hills, about her grandparents coming here to settle many years ago. There'd been wolves and cougars and bears here then, she'd said. Dillon had never seen animals like that, except in pictures. She had told him there were no cougars in the hills anymore, and the wolves and bears had disappeared too. But she suspected there were still some wild animals, perhaps even strange and unknown animals, living far back in the mountains where no one ever went.

He had spent many summers with his grandmother before his parents had returned to live in the family house. Although his grandmother was gone now, Dillon still remembered her stories. They had been full of the mysterious activities of wild geese and beavers, opossums and bears and wolves.

"Animals can talk," his grandmother had told him. "They talk quite a lot. Most people don't know this because they don't know how to listen."

When Dillon had been very young, he had believed his grandmother. He turned his head sharply as a chickadee suddenly landed on a branch overhead and began chirping to other birds in a tree nearby. Maybe animals can talk, thought Dillon, but what these birds were saying made no sense to him. He wondered what had happened to the falcon, if it had managed to get away. How could anyone mistake a person for a bird?

"It must have been an accident," he whispered softly to Mary Jane. The old dog gazed up at him with her usual mournful look. Carol's parents had warned them about hunters, but it wasn't even hunting season yet, thought Dillon. Reaching over to brush away a leaf that had fallen in Carol's hair, he closed his eyes and wished they'd never come here.

Something shuffled through the bushes on one side and Dillon opened his eyes to see a slender, brown animal poke its face into the clearing. A weasel, he thought, as the animal spotted him and slipped back into the cover of the trees.

Slowly the woods were coming back to life with the murmur of insects and the rustlings of birds and small animals. He hoped his grandmother had been right and there were no cougars left in the hills. He wasn't very familiar with real wild animals, though he'd read enough about them. He didn't think he wanted to meet any just now. At least he had Mary Jane with him. He patted the old dog who'd fallen asleep. It'd probably be awhile before help would arrive. Shifting his weight and tucking his knees up to his chin, he waited.

The afternoon passed, and the autumn sun was losing its warmth as it inched slowly westward over the tree tops. A breeze ruffled Dillon's hair and nudged fallen leaves around in little cool gusts. Dillon had not actually fallen asleep, but his thoughts had drifted off, lulled by the gently swaying branches and the many small voices of the woods blending into a quiet melody that wrapped around his memory like a forgotten lullaby.

Noticing the lengthening shadows, Dillon shook himself free of his daze. It was later than he had realized.

Maybe nobody would come before it got dark. He and Carol had hiked several miles from the main highway following an old, unused logging road. He knew he'd never be able to carry Carol up the hill and back down to the main road by himself.

He got up, flexing his legs that were stiff from sitting so long. He would have to go for help himself. Mary Jane watched as he undid the jacket he had tied around his waist by the sleeves and laid it over Carol's shoulders. He knew the old dog would stay if he told her to. His uncle had trained her very well. Though he would have liked to have Mary Jane with him, he thought someone should stay to watch over Carol.

"Stay, old girl," he said to the dog, scratching her behind the ears. "Stay with Carol. Take care of her till I get back."

Starting up the hill, he skirted the area where Carol had fallen, not wanting to see any sign of her death. Why had she done it? Why had she done such a dumb thing? He had shouted at her to come back, tried to go after her, but his jacket had caught on a bush and he'd wasted precious seconds trying to untangle himself. If only he'd reached her in time to stop her.

They'd come down the hill just a few moments before. They were going on a mission, Carol had told him when he came by her house that morning. She thought there must be a falcon's nest in the area, but so far she'd been unable to locate it. Today they would find it, she was sure. When they did, it would be their secret. They would become the falcons' guardians, keeping watch on the nest all winter and guarding the birds in the spring when the new eggs hatched.

"Secrecy is very, very important," Carol had said as they made their way up the old logging road, stepping over debris and avoiding potholes. "Falcons are the most special of all birds," she'd continued. "They almost totally died off from pesticide poisoning years ago. On top of that, people still shoot them, or capture them and sell them. We'll have to make sure nobody hurts our falcons even if we have to guard them with our own lives."

At the time, Dillon hadn't taken all this very seriously. He was not a bird fanatic. He didn't mind going out with Carol because he got to use her dad's binoculars and the hikes were okay, though he didn't really care for the pre-dawn watches she set up at a barn half a mile from her house. Those were to watch for bats as they came back before sunrise to roost all day under the rafters. Bats gave him the creeps. Carol liked them, though. Perhaps she just liked anything that could fly.

Reaching the top of a hill, Dillon looked down to where Mary Jane lay next to Carol. They looked small and peaceful lying there, as if both of them were only sleeping. Beyond them, dusky green hills rose up one after the other until, somewhere in the unseen distance, they grew into mountains.

The logging road wasn't far, but there was a stand of trees and dense underbrush to go through before he could reach it. He'd have to make good time, and even so, he figured it'd most likely be dark before he got to the main highway.

The air had grown cooler. Without his jacket, Dillon had only a T-shirt and an old, scruffy sweatshirt to keep him warm. Hunching his shoulders and moving quickly, he pushed aside branches of rustling yellow leaves, brushing wispy spider webs from his face as he went. In the gathering dusk, he peered into the shadows between the trees, shadows that grew deeper by the minute with the setting sun.

His mother had told him that when he was much younger he had had to sleep with a light on because he was so afraid of the dark. Otherwise, she said, he'd have bad dreams and wake his parents up crawling into bed with them. He couldn't remember any of that, and he certainly wasn't afraid of the dark anymore. Just the same, he would be very glad to be home.

The road seemed to be farther than he remembered. He was pretty sure he was going in the right direction, but it was hard to tell one tree from the next and he couldn't recall any distinguishing landmarks. The truth was, he hadn't paid all that much attention. Carol had always been the guide, the one who knew which way to go. Without her, he felt uncertain and a little lost. He tried not to think about her. It was easier to imagine she was only sleeping, though he knew that wasn't really true. But right now he had to concentrate on getting home and not getting lost.

Somewhere nearby an owl hooted. He thought he heard shuffling sounds behind him, but when he stopped, the sounds stopped too, so perhaps he was only hearing himself. As he made his way around a large tree, he caught his foot on an exposed root and stumbled, grabbing at a low, thin branch to keep from falling. The branch snapped in two and Dillon landed on his side among dead leaves and damp earth.

He shook his head and wiped the dirt from his hands, then rubbed his forehead where it felt as if he'd bumped it. He couldn't feel any lump, and his ankle seemed all right when he moved it. He glanced around at the darkening trees and started to get up.

Just then a flash of something bright caught his eye. He tried to peer through the swaying branches in front of him as another flash came and went, disappearing behind the shifting green leaves stirred up by the evening breeze. He crawled forward to push aside some branches and found himself staring across several feet of space directly into the eyes of a falcon.

Dillon froze. He had never wanted to admit it to Carol, but he was afraid of birds. Not the chirpy little things that hung about in the garden at his house; those were okay. But the bigger ones—the crows and geese and owls and hawks Carol was forever in search of. He was very afraid of large birds.

Beneath the unwavering gaze of the falcon, Dillon slowly sat up. At any other time, he would have backed away as fast as he could, but this was the bird Carol had been searching for. Cautiously, he took a closer look at the falcon, stranded on the ground with one drooping wing. So, the hunters had hit it after all, thought

Dillon, but only the wing as far as he could tell. Maybe they would have killed it if Carol hadn't intervened.

They had only just spotted the falcon, sitting high in a tree back up the hill they'd just come down. It must have been there all along, silently watching them. Then, in a split second it had tumbled out of sight, just as the air ripped and vibrated in the wake of a shot. Carol had torn up the hill, waving her arms and yelling, "Don't shoot!" Perhaps they hadn't heard her. Perhaps they hadn't even seen her. A second shot missed its target, putting an end to Carol's life halfway through her twelfth year.

So now Dillon faced the falcon alone. Peregrine, Carol had called it. She had even known its Latin name. *Falco peregrinus,* she had whispered like some magical charm as they searched the wooded hills. The name meant traveler, wanderer, pilgrim. Dillon didn't need much knowledge of birds to know that this particular traveler would travel no more without help.

CHAPTER 2

There wasn't much time. In the waning light it was getting more difficult to make out the shape of things under the trees. Dillon had to decide what to do about the falcon. Carol, of course, would have known what to do. Once they had found a gull with a mangled foot, and Carol had managed to wrap it in her jacket so they could carry it home.

But Dillon had no jacket to wrap around the falcon. He wondered why the bird didn't try to get away from him. Wild birds were supposed to be afraid of people, he thought, but the falcon just stood there, watching him intently with its dark eyes.

Once, when Dillon's uncle had taken him to the county fair, he'd seen several people with wild hawks and eagles and owls perched on their arms. All the birds had been injured, mostly by hunters, the people had said. The owl was blind in one eye and the other birds couldn't fly. The people had on long, thick leather gloves to protect their arms from the birds' talons.

Dillon took a deep breath and glanced nervously around. Maybe it wasn't such a good idea to try to capture the bird himself. Maybe it would stay there while he went for help and someone else could come and get it. He looked at the falcon with its injured wing dragging on the ground. The bird looked steadily back at him with a keen, almost hypnotic gaze, making it hard for Dillon to look away.

"A bird that can't fly is as good as a dead bird," he remembered his grandmother saying one day when an injured crow had wandered into the yard. Unable to fly, the falcon would be an easy target for any hunter, animal or human. He'd been unable to save Carol. The very least he could do was to try to save the falcon. It's what she would have done.

Reaching down, he took off one of his shoes and then the sock. With the falcon following each movement, he put the shoe back on his bare foot and wound the long, thick sock several times around his left arm above the wrist, using his teeth to help tie it in place. Next he unfastened the leather belt that had belonged to his uncle. It was too big for him but he wore it anyway because he liked the silver buckle shaped like the head of a wolf. He unsnapped the buckle and put it in his pocket. Then he wrapped the belt around his arm over the sock and fastened it. It wasn't as good as the gloves the people at the fair had worn, but for lack of anything better, it would have to do.

The owl hooted again as Dillon gritted his teeth and began crawling toward the bird. He was within arm's reach of it when he started shaking. Up close he could see the notch in the falcon's beak and the long, sharp talons on its feet. It was strong enough to tear the flesh from the bones of its prey, and Dillon's own fear of birds was growing to the point of panic. He shut his eyes tight to hold back the tears that had crept into them and breathed deeply to stop the trembling in his arms.

With his eyes shut he could see Carol again, running up the hill. "Don't shoot! Don't shoot! Don't shoot!" Her words echoed in his head as he opened his eyes and held out his arm to the bird.

"Please," he said between clenched teeth. He felt afraid and foolish too, because he knew he wasn't good at talking to animals, at "aahing" and "cooing" as if they were babies, the way other people did.

"Please," he repeated in a whisper, moving his arm closer to the bird.

The falcon put its head down and pecked at the belt. Dillon shut his eyes, trying to still the trembling in his arms, and turned his face away in case the bird should decide to attack him. He felt something heavy and opened his eyes slowly to look cautiously down the length of his arm.

The falcon was perched near his wrist, gripping the belt with its talons. It turned its head sideways to watch him with one sharp eye just as the sky suddenly erupted in a burst of harsh cries. From the west came wave after wave of crows. Dillon looked up at a multitude of dark bodies and rushing wings, piercing the air with their raucous voices as they headed home to roost for the night.

Amid the din of flapping wings, he got carefully to his feet. The bird appeared calm yet watchful, holding itself still except for little movements of its head as it kept an eye on him. Dillon stared at the bird in amazement. It was almost as if it had been expecting his arrival and help, so easily did it take to his arm. There was little time to wonder, though, at the bird's behavior. It was getting dark and he could hardly see the trees in front of him. With the bird leaning forward on his arm as if to point the way, they reached the road just as the last of the crows' voices faded over the hills.

Holding the falcon at arm's length from him, Dillon made his way carefully down the road. The light was so poor he could just barely make out the rocks and bits of broken branches that littered the ground and the potholes that seemed to crop up suddenly in front of his feet. His arm ached with the weight of the bird, and he began peering into the gloom for a branch the right size to use as a walking stick.

Along the side of the road he found a thick, slightly curved branch, weather-beaten and smooth. As he was brushing the dirt from it, he remembered the pocket-size flashlight he'd picked up in a junk store a few days before. Had he stuffed it in his pockets with the other things he usually carried with him?

He rested his left hand on the stick to ease the weight of the bird and searched his pockets with the other hand while the falcon watched. He hoped he hadn't left it in his jacket. It had only a weak beam, but anything would be welcome now. With relief his fingers closed on the thin, flat shape and he pulled it out, pointing its skinny beam on the road ahead.

The sun was gone, trailing gray twilight in its wake. With the help of the flashlight, Dillon at least avoided stumbling, though he had to move slowly since the light didn't reach very far. On either side of the road trees stretched darkly upwards, leaving a narrow strip of sky overhead. He heard the owl again and another further off, answering it.

Using the walking stick to help support the bird's weight, he picked his way cautiously in the dark, wondering how long it would take to get home. His parents were bound to worry if he wasn't there for dinner. He had no way of knowing how late it was, since his watch was spread out in little pieces on the workbench in the garage at home. It had broken, and he wanted to see if could fix it himself before getting a new one. He'd found a couple of old watches in the junk tins and was going to see if he could put together one good one from them all.

As Carol had loved hawks, Dillon loved junk. He collected it. Anything might come in handy sometime so he saved everything. He could spend hours at a time taking apart some old, broken thing, trying to figure out how it worked.

The watch project was proving difficult because all the tiny pieces were so hard to work with. He was thinking about it as he walked along, wishing his uncle were still alive to help him. His uncle could fix anything. Dillon wondered where he could get a set of small jeweler's tools and tried not to think about the pain in his arm and legs and the chill that was seeping through his clothes. He was concentrating hard on the problem so he wouldn't worry about Carol and Mary Jane left back there alone. Overhead long branches swayed darkly against the gray sky.

The road turned sharply to the right, climbing a short, steep hill. Dillon stopped and looked around. He didn't remember this. He thought the road should wind steadily downhill until it hit the main highway. Could he have come out onto some other road after rescuing the falcon?

He went on a little further until he got to the top of the rise, from where he could see that the road did go downhill again. If he had somehow gone the wrong way, it was a little late to go back now and search for the right road. He doubted he'd be able to find it in the dark, anyway.

Tired and shivering, he looked out over the dark, forested hills. The first stars of the night were visible, lone beacons blinking in the distance. The landscape appeared different to him. In the daytime, he thought, you should be able to see bare patches on the farther hills, where the trees had been logged. Now, in the dark, it looked unfamiliar, like one vast, continuous forest stretching as far as the eye could see.

The falcon shone grayish blue in the pale light, its eyes gleaming like two earthbound stars as it gazed into the darkness ahead of them. Dillon held his arm straight out, keeping as much distance as he could between himself and the bird. Though afraid of it, he had to admit he was a little relieved at not being totally alone. Unlike him, the bird was at home here, far from the lights and traffic.

Hoping he was going in the right direction, Dillon continued down the hill. There really wasn't much choice, and the road was bound to come out somewhere. He told himself it couldn't be much farther to go before he'd find someone, anyone, to help.

One by one more stars gathered overhead as the road rose again then dipped back down, winding its way through the trees. Dillon could still see no sign of the highway. The falcon felt heavier and even looked bigger, perched on his arm in the dark. At a turn in the road he stopped, leaning heavily on the stick to rest his arm from the weight of the bird. The sound of his own feet kicking up pebbles and small rocks gave way to other sounds as soon as he stopped.

Rustlings and shufflings came and went in the shadows on either side. When he pointed the flashlight in their direction, the sounds stopped, only to resume as soon as he turned away. He looked around nervously, feeling like he'd stumbled into some foreign place where he was perhaps tolerated but not trusted. It was as if the night was listening and waiting for him to pass before going about its business.

What if his grandmother had been right and animals did talk? What were they saying now, he wondered, whispering to each other in the dark? And what kind of animals were they? Bats? Were the trees full of bats, talking to each other in voices he couldn't hear? He shook himself. He must be awfully tired to be thinking this way.

The road became narrower and deeply rutted. It was now barely wide enough for one vehicle to pass. This change in the road was another thing he didn't remember; the logging road had been wider and not quite so rugged. He would have been more worried about being lost if he hadn't been so tired. All he could think of was to keep moving until he got to some place he knew.

Suddenly the falcon began shifting nervously on his arm. For some time it had sat very still, but now it was restless and straining forward, turning its head from side to side. It grew more and more agitated, peering into the darkness ahead of them. Dillon's fear of birds came flooding back. Would it attack him, he wondered? Would it reach out with that sharp beak and get him in the face?

The falcon sent Dillon one piercing glance before turning away from him. It opened its good wing and began flapping furiously in the direction of the woods, all the time holding tight to Dillon's arm with its feet as if to take him with it. Dillon was being pulled off the road, cool air rushing over his face from the force of the bird's crippled flight, powerful in spite of the injured wing.

He couldn't understand what had come over the bird. He dug in his heels, trying to keep on the road. He was not very tall and was a little on the lean side, so it took all the strength he had to try to counter the falcon's flight. His arm ached as the bird clutched him tighter, drawing him toward the woods where he knew he'd never be able to find his way.

"Are you crazy?" he shouted at the bird. "Stop it, you crazy, stupid bird. Stop it!" he yelled as he gripped his left arm with his other hand, trying to pull the frantic bird back onto the road.

Then he heard it. From down the road came the low hum of an approaching truck. It grew louder and louder, the rumbling and rattling of its engine echoing eerily over the dark hills. Beneath his shoes, Dillon could feel the ground vibrating as the truck drew nearer, the racket of its motor unnaturally loud and menacing in the otherwise still night.

Suddenly Dillon heard the sharp snap of a fallen branch cracking under a wheel. The sound sent a tremor through his body, piercing the night sky like the sound of the gunshot had pierced the peacefulness of the afternoon.

"Hunters!" he whispered.

Dillon didn't stop to think. He didn't stop to wonder why hunters would be out at night. All he knew was that he didn't want to be caught in the glare of the headlights, alone on the road. Perhaps the falcon's fear had affected him. Carol had said that people shoot falcons or capture them to sell. The dark hills and dense shadows made Dillon feel he was worlds from home, from safety. He gave in to the falcon, letting it lead him off the road and deep into the dark interior of the towering trees.

CHAPTER 3

Pushing away branches that struck against his face with his free hand, Dillon fled from the sound of the truck. The night was shattered with noise and confusion as he plunged through the woods, tripping over roots and things he couldn't see. He stumbled blindly on, the flashlight dancing erratically over the trees. Dark shapes rushed past him and leafy arms snatched at his clothing as he was led deeper into the forest by the falcon's wild flight.

Finally the bird came to a stop, panting heavily, and Dillon collapsed against the trunk of an old tree, hanging his head between his knees to catch his breath. In the distance he could hear the truck moving slowly up the road, the sound fading away as his breathing returned to normal and the night closed in around him.

His sleeve was torn where it had snagged on a tree limb, and bits of leaves and broken twigs stuck to his clothes. He shone the flashlight on the falcon to see if it was all right. It shook itself, fluffing up its feathers, and huddled on Dillon's arm, blinking in the light. Its injured wing looked ragged, hanging pathetically at its side. There were dark splotches on it; probably blood, thought Dillon.

He rested his forehead on his knees. He didn't know what had come over him. Maybe the truck was only someone coming to help. He couldn't know that for sure, though, without running the risk of showing himself to whoever it was. He wasn't sure he wanted to do that. Dillon shivered. He and the falcon would just rest awhile, then make their way back to the road.

The toes on his sockless foot were growing numb, and the old sweatshirt was not nearly enough protection from the night air. He turned off the flashlight, worried about wearing out the batteries, then thought about turning it back on again. He wasn't a little kid anymore, he told himself, and he'd need the light to find his way back to the road. The falcon had good hearing; it had proved that. If there was anything to be afraid of, it would let him know.

In the dark he could hear whisperings and rustlings, closer now than when he was on the road. Forests didn't really sleep. There were animals that came out at night to forage for food. Dillon tried to remember their names, but he was too cold and tired to think anymore. Curling up against the large, exposed roots spreading out like arms from the base of the tree, he closed his eyes. Sleep came almost at once, and his thoughts drifted away from trucks and hunters and the snapping sound of things breaking.

Dillon shifted his head, still asleep, covering his face with his hand. He swatted at the air, as if to push something away. Slowly he opened his eyes and blinked at the yellowish light spreading softly around him and scattering the shadows to show the falcon still perched on his arm. He had forgotten about time and place and what had brought him there. Hanging between dreaming and waking, he felt very comfortable curled up between the smooth old roots.

Then he noticed that the light had become somewhat brighter, as if it had moved closer to him. Gazing into it, he thought he could see a face like that of a dog, like Mary Jane only bigger, heavier. He sat up with a jolt, fully awake. Or was he? Sometimes he had dreams in which he knew he was dreaming but couldn't stop the dream from happening so he had to go along with it. That must be what was happening now, he thought, because the face in front of him couldn't possibly belong to a dog.

It was too large, for one thing, more like a bear only too small for a bear. Its shaggy, dark fur was broken by a pale white band across its forehead. Down its sides ran two broad, yellowish stripes ending in a thick, bushy tail. Around its muzzle the fur was mottled with gray, like that of an old dog. Two brown eyes watched him.

A wolverine, thought Dillon. He'd seen pictures of wolverines and knew they lived alone, far away from people. His grandmother had thought that wolverines were highly intelligent. She'd said that hunters didn't like them because they would steal the bait right out of their traps.

Padding silently around the tree, the wolverine moved in a circle, examining Dillon and the falcon carefully while pausing now and then to sniff the ground. It was a very odd thing to run across a wolverine, thought Dillon. They were supposed to live only in wild places. What was this one doing in the hills near home? It seemed to be quite old, judging by its slow, stiff steps and the stoop of its shoulders.

When it came to a stop in front of him, Dillon saw that the pale, yellowish light was coming from above the wolverine's head. Leaning closer, he made out the shape of a small animal perched between the wolverine's ears. It was about the size of a chipmunk but had the dark ears and eyes and the long, thin face of an opossum. Mary Jane had quite a reputation for hunting opossums in her younger days. But this one was certainly much smaller than any living opossum, thought Dillon, and its eyes seemed almost human as it leaned forward to look at him. In its tiny outstretched arm it held a miniature lantern.

Dillon smiled. He didn't usually have dreams like this. Usually his dreams were confused and hard to remember, or sometimes full of shapeless things he didn't want to remember. The events of the afternoon were forgotten as he leaned back against the tree and gazed at the creatures gazing back at him.

The wolverine shifted its weight to sit down, and it was then that Dillon noticed the third creature. A small, dark bat with huge ears was hanging upside down from the wolverine's tail. It was so small, Dillon wouldn't have noticed it at all if it weren't for the three odd white spots on its back that looked like a face—two eyes and a mouth, huddled upside down in the fur of the wolverine's tail. It flew off to hang from a nearby branch as the old animal settled down on his hind legs.

Sitting beneath the halo of light from the lantern, the wolverine sighed. He moved his head slowly to one side and then the other, listening and sniffing lightly at the air. Then he brought his gaze around to Dillon and rested it there.

"What brings you here?" said the wolverine at last, with a voice so deep and low it could have been mistaken for the wind.

Dillon tried to speak but found his throat too dry to form words. The lantern swayed as the opossum leaned forward, waiting for Dillon's reply. Hanging from the branch, the bat's face looked very tiny, dwarfed as it was by the incredibly large ears that were almost as big as its body. It too, listened.

"I, um, I don't know," said Dillon, after clearing his throat several times. He eyed the bat nervously, hoping it would stay up in the tree.

The wolverine looked down at the ground, then slowly back at Dillon.

"Who shot Peregrine?" the old animal asked with that strange voice that was more like something felt than something heard.

Dillon looked at the falcon. She was calmly following the movements of the lantern and didn't seem at all alarmed by the three creatures. He took this as a good sign, since she knew the night and the woods better than he did.

"I don't know," he replied.

"He doesn't know much, does he?" said the opossum in a loud whisper, speaking into the wolverine's ear.

"He's very young," said a squeaky, high-pitched voice. The bat shifted her position on the branch. "He's very young to know much," she added.

"Yes, he's very young," agreed the wolverine.

All three animals regarded Dillon with a knowing air, as if there were no point in saying more. Dillon felt he had to defend himself; he wasn't all that young.

"It might have been a couple of boys I saw," he said. "They had shotguns and came over to see what had happened."

"Do you know these boy-hunters?" asked the wolverine. "Are they friends of yours?"

"No," said Dillon. "I don't know who they are."

"Then what are you doing with Peregrine?" asked the wolverine.

"I found her by accident," said Dillon.

Off in the distance a wolf howled, or maybe it was a coyote. Dillon wasn't sure; he'd never heard either before. His grandmother would have known the difference, he thought.

The wolverine looked solemnly at Dillon.

"So you decided to rescue Peregrine," he said. "Why? What does one more dead bird mean to you?"

"I had to rescue her," said Dillon. "I couldn't leave her alone. She's hurt."

The wolverine gazed at him thoughtfully. The other animals were silent. The masked face of a raccoon appeared at the edge of the light cast by the lantern. Ignoring them, it sniffed around awhile before shuffling back into the surrounding gloom.

The wolverine's questions made Dillon uneasy. He seemed to be on trial, yet he didn't know what he was guilty of. If he had done something wrong, it hadn't been intentional.

"I rescued the falcon because it's what Carol would have done," he explained. "She loved hawks."

"Who is Carol?" asked the wolverine.

"She's my friend," said Dillon. "We were trying to find the falcon's nest so we could protect it."

The thought of Carol brought a sharp pang. Carol would have known how to handle this. She could have explained everything to the wolverine, who seemed to think that he was to blame for the falcon's injured wing.

"Where is your friend?" the wolverine asked. "Why isn't she with you?"

"She's dead," said Dillon, clenching his jaw and staring down at his feet. He was not going to cry, not now, in front of strangers.

The wolverine waited a moment before going on.

"How did she die?" he asked gently.

"She was shot," said Dillon slowly, looking up at the wolverine. "It was an accident, I guess. They meant to shoot the bird."

The wolverine closed his eyes, turning his face into the breeze that was setting the branches to sway in the darkness outside the small circle of light.

"Poor Carol," said the opossum, covering his eyes with a tiny paw. "Poor, poor Carol."

Dillon heard the sound of Carol's voice again as she ran up the hill and the deafening shot that had turned everything inside out. He looked around at the strange place he had come to, stumbled into actually, running blindly from the road with only the falcon as a guide. Dark and silent, the place seemed very distant from where he had started out when he had left his friends to get help. He worried about Carol and Mary Jane, left alone in the dark at the foot of the hill.

"It's been a long time since any human came here," said the wolverine, looking again at Dillon, his clothes torn and dirty from the flight through the woods. "Used to be you would run across a human now and then," the wolverine continued. "But that was long ago. Nobody comes here much anymore. Seems they've all forgotten this place."

Dillon looked up at the wolverine. The old animal had a faraway look in his eyes. Years ago, when Dillon had listened to his grandmother's stories, she had looked just like that, as if gazing back in time.

"What place is this?" he asked.

The wolverine didn't answer right away. Dillon

thought he hadn't been heard and was about to ask again when the wolverine spoke.

"Oh, the name doesn't matter," he said. "Sometimes a human will stumble in here by accident, lost and afraid. Sometimes they find their way home again and think it was all a dream. Do dreams have names?" asked the wolverine, not really expecting an answer.

Dillon frowned. No, he thought, dreams don't have names, and he was beginning to feel uncomfortable in this one. He needed to do something to break the spell.

He stood up, leaning on the walking stick. The falcon still gripped his arm, having shown no inclination to perch anywhere else. She watched Dillon as he gazed around at the dark woods.

"Well, I better get going," Dillon said. "I've got to get home and get help for Carol. Good-bye."

He turned to retrace the route he and the bird had taken, anxious to leave the strange animals behind and somehow wake up back on the road to home.

"Oh, you can't go that way," cried the opossum. "You can't go back."

"No, there's no going back," said the bat, gesturing emphatically with her leathery wings.

Dillon shone the flashlight around at a thick wall of brambles. He was standing at the edge of a small meadow. Just then, the moon breached the top of the trees on the other side of the clearing, spreading a pale light as it climbed the sky. Beyond the border of twisting brambles, Dillon could make out the dark forms of tall hemlock and spruce, their needle-laden branches swaying high overhead.

These were not the hills he and Carol had hiked into. Here there were no silvery trees with yellowing leaves. Dillon realized with alarm that he was beyond the hills and well into the mountains. How, he asked himself, could he have gotten so far from the road?

He walked along the edge of the meadow, looking for a break in the border, but the brambles grew so close and thick there seemed to be no way through them. The tree he'd fallen asleep under stood alone in the clearing, its branches beginning halfway up the trunk, high above his head. He sat down again on one of the roots, facing the wolverine.

"I need to get home," said Dillon.

"Yes, you do," said the wolverine.

Dillon pushed the toe of his shoe at a clump of skinny, bell-topped mushrooms growing at his feet.

"Is there a way out of here?" he asked.

"There is a way through here," answered the wolverine.

"How do I find it?" asked Dillon.

The wolverine sighed again. "It's not easy," he said.

"No, it's not," agreed the opossum, shaking his head slowly.

"You can get lost if you're not careful," said the bat, dropping down from the branch to circle above their heads.

"I'll be careful," said Dillon, trying not to betray how nervous he felt with the bat flying around. "Just tell me which way to go."

The wolverine rose stiffly to his feet. Dillon ducked as the bat passed close to his head before landing on the wolverine's tail, where she resumed her upside-down position.

"We'll walk with you to the other side of the mountain," said the wolverine. "From there you can see the way home, but you'll have to go the rest of the way by yourself."

"Is it far?" Dillon asked, following the others as they crossed the meadow.

"It can be," said the wolverine. "With luck, you might be home by morning."

Approaching the border, the wolverine and his companions slipped through a shadow in the wall of brambles. Following close behind them, Dillon saw they were on a narrow path leading into the forest. He hadn't been able to see any break in the wall until the wolverine passed through it, and when he turned to look behind him the path had disappeared again, swallowed up in the dark mass of brambles.

Leaving the path, they entered the hushed interior of the forest. A thick canopy of branches overhead prevented any moonlight from penetrating down to them. Only the opossum's lantern illuminated their way, allowing Dillon to see the fern-covered forest floor in front of them.

Weaving a trail through the trees, they made their way slowly around the side of the mountain. The place seemed old to Dillon, like the wolverine. Tree trunks cracked with thick bark and nearly covered with moss disappeared into the gloom above. Pine needles littered the ground, muffling the sound of their feet.

Suddenly two deer appeared ahead of them. Startled by the light, they blinked and backed away. Dillon could see only their eyes glistening in the dark as he passed. Were there other eyes, further back in the shadows, watching them? He kept close to the wolverine, reassured by the old animal's ease at finding his way through the nighttime landscape.

The soft swoosh of wings brushed the air as an owl swept down from above, keeping ahead of them for a short distance until it veered sharply to the side and disappeared. Up ahead the night sky slowly began to appear between breaks in the trees, and soon they came out onto a rocky clearing overlooking a valley.

Dillon stopped, stunned by the view before him. He had never seen anything like this. A huge, brilliant moon hung high overhead, crowning an immense sky alive with millions of shimmering stars. Beneath the sparkling dome, a vast valley stretched from the base of the mountain, rolling gently downwards and dipping around little hills until it unfolded onto a nearly flat plain. Thick growing woods gave way to clusters of trees like leafy islands in a sea of grass. Still further out, the trees were few and far between as the valley reached into the distance to meet the foothills of a remote range of dim mountains. To one side, a river flowed unseen, told only by the dense growth along its banks as it snaked its way across the length of the valley.

The wolverine sat down, sending the bat scurrying to another perch. Using a boulder for a seat, Dillon gazed across to the distant mountains silhouetted in the night sky. For the first time he felt content to stay where he was, all thoughts of home temporarily vanishing in the star-washed landscape. Leaning forward on his arm, the falcon pushed her head into the wind as it ruffled the feathers down her back. Her dark eyes absorbed each surrounding detail with the familiarity of a native.

"There's a narrow trail down from here," said the wolverine. "Follow the river, use its banks for cover, and you should be able to make it safely across the valley. Then you must cross to the other side of the mountains."

"What's beyond the mountains?" asked Dillon.

"Sunrise," said the wolverine.

Dillon looked at the wolverine.

"I mean," he said, "what lies beyond the mountains?"

This time the wolverine looked at Dillon.

"Your home lies beyond the mountains," he said.

Dillon was confused. He seemed to have lost all sense of direction since finding the falcon. He couldn't understand how he'd come to be where he was, let alone that his home should lie so far away, across wide and unfamiliar territory.

"Humans have forgotten so much," said the wolverine, noting Dillon's confusion. "Behind us lies the sunset," the wolverine explained, looking up at the mountain they had just crossed. Then he pointed to the valley below and the dim line of mountains beyond it. "Over there, on the other side of those mountains, lies the sunrise. Between the two there is always a valley.

If you want to be home by morning, you'll have to cross the valley and head toward sunrise. There is no other way."

"All right," said Dillon, rubbing his forehead. There was nothing to do but give in to the wolverine's logic, strange as it was. Nothing that had happened so far made much sense to him anyway, and he had no better idea of which way to go.

Getting to his feet, Dillon stepped to the edge of the rock-strewn clearing, using the walking stick to steady himself as he peered over. From where he stood, he could see the beginning of the trail the wolverine had mentioned. The mountains looked a long way off, and he wondered what the wolverine had meant by needing the cover along the banks of the river. He turned back to the others.

The opossum seemed nervous, fidgeting in his seat between the wolverine's ears. The bat had crawled up to the old animal's shoulder, where Dillon could hear her speaking.

"We should warn him," said the bat.

"Yes, we should warn him," agreed the opossum, nodding his head vigorously. "What he doesn't know might hurt him."

"After all, he is so young," said the bat.

"And he is not a night creature, like us," added the opossum.

"That's right," agreed the bat. "He doesn't know the shadows and the hidden places like we do."

"What are you talking about?" asked Dillon.

The wolverine shook his head slightly, hushing the others.

"When you cross the valley, there is one thing you should watch out for," he said, turning to look at Dillon.

Before he could go on, the bat flew up above Dillon's head, flapping in circles.

"Beware of the shadow that moves on the wind," warned the bat.

The opossum appeared even more agitated now, the lantern swaying in his trembling arm.

"The one that rises in a fume of smoke," said the opossum.

"Run!" said the bat. "Run if you see the Face in the Smoke!"

CHAPTER 4

As if in answer to the bat's warning, a dark cloud swept across the sky, trailing its shadow along the valley below and momentarily blotting out the moon. When it had passed, Dillon repeated his question.

"What are you talking about?" he asked.

The wolverine got up and walked slowly over to where Dillon stood. The valley glowed softly, trees and rocky outcroppings outlined in the silvery light of the moon.

"We're talking about the valley between sunset and sunrise," replied the wolverine, looking at the wide expanse below them. "The valley you must cross to get home." He turned to Dillon. "Sleeping animals find shelter in its shadows, but not all that lie in the shadows are asleep." As the wolverine spoke, a golden eagle glided down from the top of the mountain behind them, its feathers gleaming in the moonlight. Floating on air, it dipped and turned down into the valley.

"I don't understand," said Dillon as he watched the eagle become a speck in the distance.

The wolverine paused before going on.

"The valley is very old," he explained slowly. "Older than anyone can remember. Everything has a place here: all that is beautiful, sad, welcomed, or feared. Every traveler that passes through trails his own shadow of memories and dreams. You can cross it safely, as others have before you, but you should be careful."

"Yes," said the opossum, nodding his head. "You should be careful."

The bat left the wolverine and crawled across the ground toward Dillon, who looked down in horror as the tiny animal started climbing up his leg. Carol would have called him a baby to be afraid of something so small, but he couldn't help it; he had never liked bats. He fought against the urge to swat the bat away, standing very still as she made her way up to his shoulder.

"Take my advice," said the bat, speaking in Dillon's ear. "Stick to the river and stay low. If you're lucky, it won't see you."

"What won't see me?" asked Dillon slowly, trying not to look at the bat.

"The Face in the Smoke," the bat whispered.

"The one who never sleeps," said the opossum, shivering.

"I've seen it," said the bat. "I've seen it down on the plain, wrapped in a shroud of soot and smoke."

The wolverine hushed the others. "Opossum and Bat are small and easily alarmed," he said to Dillon. "All of us become alarmed sometimes at things we don't know. Being alarmed keeps us from being careless. Fear, though, can paint a face on anything."

The wolverine looked at Dillon, who still failed to understand what they were talking about and wondered if animals always talk in such a roundabout manner.

"The Face they speak of," the wolverine went on, "really has no face at all. It prowls the night like a phantom, hiding its hollow eyes behind a mask."

The wind darted around them, tugging at Dillon's clothes. He shivered, telling himself it was because of the wind and the bat's proximity and not because of talk of some smoky phantom.

"Those of us who live on the edge of the valley know that all things have their place and time," said the wolverine. "Even death has its place."

Dillon didn't think he agreed, at least not totally. Maybe some things had their place and time but he didn't see how anyone could believe that Carol's place and time to die was a sun-drenched autumn hillside. It just wasn't fair.

The wolverine moved to the head of the trail leading down from the mountain. "If you want to be home by morning, you had better not delay," he said to Dillon. "There's danger in any journey, but Peregrine will help you. She brought you safely this far, she can help you safely home, if you listen to her warnings."

Dillon wondered if the falcon's panic and flight at the sound of the approaching truck was what the wolverine meant by warnings. Could the old animal have known about that? He was about to ask when the bat flew off his shoulder and fluttered around in front of him.

"I will guide you down the trail," she said. "It's steep and dark, and you might lose your way."

"I have a flashlight," said Dillon, not anxious for the bat's company.

"That silly thing?" said the bat. "It will hardly do more than let the Face know where you are."

"Bat doesn't need eyes to see," said the opossum. "She speaks to the night and listens to its echoes. She knows where everything is."

Dillon thought he saw the wolverine smile. He hoped the old animal hadn't guessed the real reason he wasn't anxious to have the bat accompany him.

"You're lucky to have Bat for a guide," said the wolverine. "The night is no barrier to her."

Dillon crossed the edge of the clearing to the trail. It was a narrow path, disappearing into the trees to come out somewhere far below. Ahead of him flew the bat, the white spots on her back standing out clearly in the night, like a tiny face bobbing up and down in the air. At least it was better to have the creature in front of him than clinging to his shoulder, he thought. He took a few steps down the trail then hesitated, turning to look back at the others. Unsure of what lay ahead of him, he was reluctant to leave the company of the wolverine.

"My legs are too old for the steep journeys," said the wolverine gently. "You have to go by yourself."

Dillon still hesitated, finding it hard to take the next step leading down into the unknown valley. The wind blew around him, sweeping down from the mountain and pushing him in the direction of the trail. The night seemed endless and the distant mountains too far away. His legs were tired, and the falcon weighed heavily on his aching arm. The thought of the long journey ahead made him wish he was already home, asleep in his own bed.

He looked at the wolverine, wanting to speak but unable to find the right words. He didn't want to go on by himself. He was too tired and cold and lonely, and he didn't know his way through this strange place. He didn't want to meet any phantoms, with or without faces. He didn't see how a tiny bat and an injured bird could help him or guide him. The wolverine claimed he was too old to go any further, and Carol was dead. Carol, who had always known which way to go, was dead.

Dillon felt the anger rising in his throat, anger at everything that had happened. He was angry at being tired and lost, angry at his own fear, and angry at the boys whose aim was so bad they shouldn't even have been allowed to go hunting. It was the falcon they'd been aiming at, the falcon who should have died. Not Carol.

The falcon was watching him closely. Jaw set tight, he stared back at her, wanting to hate her and blame her for everything that had happened. He wanted to toss her away, turn his back on all the animals, and find his own way home.

"What would your friend have done if she had lived?" asked the wolverine.

Dillon stared at the old animal. How was it that the wolverine seemed to be able to get right inside his thoughts? He turned away and looked out over the dark mountainside below. He was tired of this dream. All he wanted was to be home.

As he stood there, angry but uncertain of what to do, he caught the streak of a falling star out of the corner of his eye. He looked up as it arched across the sky, burning a brief and brilliant trail before disappearing in the vastness of space. Following almost immediately, another star shot past the moon, its fleeting radiance gone as suddenly as it had appeared.

Dillon looked away. Somewhere deep in the back of his eyes a star was slowly falling, weaving threads of light through his flustered, tired feelings. The anger drained from his face. He couldn't hate the bird. It wasn't her fault. She had done nothing but sit in a tree. What had followed could not be undone.

He took a deep breath, letting the air out again slowly. There was no going back. His voice barely audible, he thanked the wolverine for his help and started down the mountain. Just before the trail disappeared around a bend, he glanced back. Above him, the wolverine and opossum sat motionless in the small circle of light, watching Dillon's descent into the valley.

The trail was narrow and very steep. It zigzagged down the side of the mountain, cutting through densely growing trees and changing direction in sharp switchbacks. In spite of the bat's warning, Dillon used the flashlight to guide his feet along the rough, uneven ground as he kept track of the bat flying ahead, the spots on her back leading him along the dark, forested mountainside.

Now and then moonlight filtered through a thinning in the trees, illuminating the trail with a pale light. At one such place, the ground widened and the trail disappeared into a large, deep pool fed by several small waterfalls that splashed lightly down the side of the mountain, running along courses worn smooth over many years of use. On the other side of the pool, the waterfalls joined forces, becoming one cascading stream rushing downward to meet the river far below.

Dillon knelt at the edge of the pool, cupping his hand to drink. The water was clear and cold. With every sip, the exhaustion of the night faded a little. He hadn't realized how thirsty he was. He held the falcon down so she too could drink.

Reflected in moonlight, trees danced on the surface of the pool. Dillon's face appeared beneath him, his features smudged and wrinkled in the rippling mirror of water, while the falcon's shimmering image looked back at him as she drank.

Dillon aimed his flashlight into the pool, catching the darting movement of a small fish. Peering deeper, he saw shadowy forms of larger fish hanging motionless near the bottom. In the soft mud along the edge, footprints approached and retreated, traces of the presence of other animals who had come to drink.

The only way across consisted of several slippery rocks, spaced so that Dillon had to jump from one to the other. He made it without falling, aided in keeping his balance by the falcon, who flapped her wing at each jump he took.

On the other side of the pool, Dillon looked around for the bat. She was easy enough to follow when she was flying because of the marks on her back, but when she was still, her small body was impossible to pick out among the branches. A dark object flitted down from above and landed on his shoulder. The bat was just inches from his ear. He shuddered. He didn't think he'd ever get used to having the creature so close to him.

They continued on their way, the bat flying ahead again, guiding him as the trail turned sharply downward. Sometimes he would catch a glimpse of the valley between a break in the trees, the wooded path of the river standing out darkly in the moonlight. They were getting closer. As they maneuvered another switchback, Dillon spoke to the bat.

"Tell me about the Face in the Smoke," he said. "The wolverine called it a phantom. Isn't a phantom a ghost?" he asked. "Ghosts aren't real."

The bat hovered in front of Dillon. "Call it a ghost or call it anything you want, I've seen it just the same," she said.

"But ghosts aren't real," said Dillon firmly, glancing around at the dark trees and pulling himself up as tall as he could.

The bat did not answer. She flew faster until Dillon could no longer keep up. They were nearing the base of the mountain, and further along the trees opened out as the trail skirted a meadow. The bat had almost reached the meadow before she realized Dillon was no longer following her and returned to the place where she'd left him. She landed on the walking stick, below Dillon's hand.

"Phantoms are shadows of something real," she said, looking up at Dillon with small, bright eyes. She crawled closer to Dillon's hand. "I've seen the Face creeping across the plain. I've seen it suddenly dart into a bush or slip down a hole," she went on. "Wherever something dies, it appears as if from nowhere to dance over the bones."

Dillon did not really believe in ghosts, at least he didn't think he did. Only living things could hurt other living things, he thought. He tried explaining this to the bat, but she stuck to her tale with the stubbornness of one who had witnessed strange things.

"I've seen its face," she said in a whisper. "It was like

a huge death mask, gray and streaked with ashes, looming up out of the smoke with big, hollow eyes."

In spite of his claim to disbelief, Dillon felt a small prickling of fear. In this strange landscape, anything might be possible. Perhaps phantoms did prowl the night. Perhaps the shadow of death, masked and wrapped in a shapeless shroud, crept sleepless beneath the darkened sky.

They came out onto the meadow. The ground had become less steep, giving way to a gently rolling slope. On the far side of the meadow, near a border of trees, a slight movement caught Dillon's eye.

He stiffened, looking across the grassy clearing and straining until he caught another glint of movement. What had at first appeared to be a tangle of fallen branches shifted in the moonlight. They were antlers. A small group of elk were resting, nearly hidden in the grass. Without further disturbing the sleeping animals, they passed on down the trail.

As they wound their way through the foothills, the country grew more open and the trees farther apart. There were grassy meadows and berry bushes and a reed-choked pond on which Dillon imagined there were ducks sleeping, though he couldn't see them. He pocketed his flashlight. The bat flew on ahead of him, but he didn't really need to follow the white spots on her back anymore. Bright and full, the moon gave enough light to see by.

They rounded a broad bend in the trail and Dillon heard the rushing sound of water flowing over rocks.

Abruptly the trail came to an end in a small, sandy patch at the river's edge. Dillon sat down on the soft sand, leaning his back against a large boulder that jutted up out of the water onto the bank. He rested his arm in his lap so that the falcon's head was only inches from his own. He had grown accustomed to her weight on his arm and no longer thought about her sharp beak or his own fear of birds.

The bat hung by her feet from a thin branch that dipped out over the water. Not far from Dillon's shoes the river idled in a shallow pool. Farther out, though, it rushed by over a rocky bed, its current deep and swift where it cut its way between huge, submerged boulders.

"I've been thinking," said the bat, rocking back and forth on the branch. "Maybe I should go on with you for a bit more."

Dillon said nothing. He drew little circles and swirls in the sand with the walking stick while he waited for the bat to continue.

"I know where hiding places are, if we should need them," continued the bat. She left the branch and landed on the boulder above his head.

Dillon didn't know what to say. As long as the bat stayed several feet away from him, he was okay. But she had a way of getting too close whenever she spoke, as she was doing now.

"We'll be all right," said Dillon, including the falcon when he spoke of himself. "It shouldn't be too hard to follow the river."

"No, it shouldn't," said the bat slowly, growing quiet.

Leaves washed by on the water, whirling around in places where eddies had formed. The wind came and went in gusts, rippling the surface of the shallow water near Dillon's feet. An owl started calling, back up the trail behind them. Just then a stronger gust of wind shook the trees on the other side of the river, bending a large branch down so that it nearly touched the water before springing up again.

From the distance, where the river flowed out across the plain, a thin, high wail rose on the wind. It faded quickly, making Dillon wonder if he had heard anything at all until it came again, very faint and remote, a howl of triumph vanishing as suddenly as it had come. The falcon moved restlessly on Dillon's arm, turning her head in the direction of the sound.

"It's out on the plain," whispered the bat in Dillon's ear. "The Face is hunting tonight. You'd better hurry. Stay close to the river and hurry."

Dillon scrambled to his feet. The sound had sent a chill down his spine. He moved into the cover of trees that bordered the river, turning to call back to the bat.

"Aren't you coming?" he asked.

The bat flapped over to his shoulder, making Dillon wince as she landed.

"You didn't seem to want my help," she said.

"Well, you said you know where hiding places are," Dillon replied.

They moved quickly, the bat gripping Dillon's

sweatshirt and the falcon clutching his arm. Dillon kept his eyes straight ahead, so he wouldn't catch sight of the small bat with her enormous ears, clinging to him. Once out of the moonlight and under the trees, it was harder to see. Heeding the bat's earlier warning, Dillon didn't dare take out his flashlight now, not after hearing that distant howl. The sound of the river to his right guided him as he moved as quickly and quietly as he could down the last stretch of hillside. Ahead lay the plain and, off in the distance, the mountains yet to be crossed before he could reach sunrise.

CHAPTER 5

As the ground leveled out, the river grew wider and calmer. It was possible to walk along its narrow, grassy bank shielded from view by the cottonwood trees that bordered it on either side. Dillon slowed his pace. They had walked for sometime without hearing any more strange cries or seeing anything suspicious. Now and then he moved away from the riverside to look between breaks in the trees as they passed.

The flat plain forming the base of the valley stretched away on either side of the river. The view here was different than it had been when he'd stood on the mountain with the wolverine. The valley looked much broader and flatter, and the distant mountains seemed smaller and much farther away. The sky also appeared different. It looked incredibly high and endlessly wide and seemed to reach down to actually touch the earth at the horizon. All the trees and plants and rocks glowed so very softly it was as if another moon, deep within the earth, was lighting them from the inside too.

Once, when Dillon glanced beyond the trees, he looked up at the sky and saw the silhouetted forms of a flock of long-necked birds. Flying silently high overhead, they looked small and fairylike as they passed in front of the moon.

The bat was still clinging to his sweatshirt. "Tell me about your friend Carol," she said, her tiny voice close to Dillon's ear. "Did you know her well?"

Dillon took a few moments to answer. He supposed he knew her well. She lived just down the road. They had met the first summer he spent at his grandmother's, when they were only little kids. Even then she'd been crazy about animals, though it had been moths and butterflies and caterpillars in those days. Carol was always working on one thing or another, and he had taken to spending more and more time at her house since there weren't many other kids his age around.

"She was always very busy," Dillon told the bat. "Kind of an outdoors person." He thought for a moment. "She liked bats," he added.

"Doesn't everyone?" asked the bat.

"I don't know, I guess so." Dillon shrugged, carefully avoiding looking at the bat.

"What will you do when you get home?" the small animal asked, moving forward on Dillon's shoulder to get a better look at him.

"I suppose I'll have to tell everyone what happened," said Dillon slowly. He thought of his parents and how worried they must be that he hadn't come home yet. The thought of having to explain about his and Carol's mission to find the falcon's nest and the shooting and everything that had followed weighed heavily on Dillon. He had never before been faced with explaining anything so difficult.

The wind died down and the night grew quiet except for the incessant low whispering of the river. Sometimes Dillon had to skirt around trees whose large roots grew right out of the bank and hung in a tangled mass at the water's edge. Most of the time, though, the going was easy, and he was beginning to think that he just might make it home by morning.

The river wandered around a small hill, widening as it curved back again. The opposite bank looked like a dark smudge across the expanse of water, and the river's surface gleamed in the pale light of night, shifting from deep, dull gray to the glint of steel blue as it rippled and rolled past him. Above he could see the golden moon, surrounded by so many glittering stars it looked as if millions of tiny jewels had been thrown randomly into space. Dillon thought he had never seen a place so silently and mysteriously beautiful.

Choosing a spot where the trees were thin so he could see out over the plain, he stopped to rest. The bat hung upside down from a limb above him while he sat with his back against a tree, gazing out at the dim line of mountains in the distance. The falcon was looking out across the plain too, though she seemed intent on one particular spot. Dillon followed her gaze and saw what looked like two geese not far away from them, walking toward the mountains.

They were large, wild geese, their heads and long necks rising above the tall grass. One of them had an odd, stumbling kind of walk, as if it might be lame. The other one walked a few paces ahead, both of them moving slowly together across the plain.

"We should be going soon," said the bat from above Dillon's head. "There's still a lot of ground to cover before we reach the foothills."

"All right," said Dillon, getting slowly to his feet.

As he stood, the leading goose rose up, flying off and calling for its mate to follow. The other goose called back but remained earthbound, stumbling along as before. Dillon watched as the first bird returned, realizing the other couldn't follow, and circled overhead before landing again to walk alongside its mate.

The bat plopped down on Dillon's shoulder as he turned back to the river. Perhaps the grounded goose had broken its wing, thought Dillon, glancing at the falcon. It wasn't safe for a bird to be stuck on the ground. He looked over his shoulder at the receding figures of the geese, hoping they would make it across the open expanse safely.

A light breeze ran over the plain, tossing the branches about as it danced out over the surface of the river. The trees murmured as their leaves brushed against each other. Dillon walked along quietly, listening to the night sounds and looking up at the sky now and then, hoping to catch sight of another falling star.

He nearly tripped into a small stream appearing suddenly at his feet. It had wound its own watery trail across the plain, hidden from view by the tall grass growing along its banks. With a slight gurgling sound, it completed its journey and merged into the river.

Dillon cleared the stream with one jump, landing on the other side. As he did so, a dark brown shape scurried out of the grass several feet away and darted down the short stream bank. The sleek, wet body of a mink, startled from its nighttime foraging, looked back at Dillon and the falcon with small, shiny brown eyes before slipping quickly into the water and swimming out of sight.

Dillon was startled, too. He realized that since leaving the mountain they hadn't run across many other animals, except the geese. He had kept track of the geese, though they'd moved farther off and were a little harder to see. Still, he could follow their progress because every so often the first goose would fly up, calling for the other to follow, only to return each time and walk slowly along again beside its injured mate.

Whenever the goose flew up and its voice rang out over the plain, the falcon would rivet her gaze to the sky and scan the horizon, relaxing only when the goose returned to its mate. Dillon too would search the sky and the distant horizon, though he wasn't sure what he expected to see.

The mountains had grown larger as he and his companions crossed the plain, each step taking them closer to their destination. Since the first eerie cries, they had neither seen nor heard any sign of the smoky phantom. For a long time the bat had said nothing, though she'd been sending out signals and listening intently to the stories they brought back. In this way she was able to draw a very detailed picture of their surroundings, including things so small they couldn't be seen in the dim light of night.

As they approached close enough to the foothills to be able to make out the forms of trees and scrubby bushes, it was the bat who first noticed the dark shape slipping down the side of the nearest hill. It slunk down from the trees and rocks and disappeared into the grass, the bat following its progress with her large, thin ears.

The two geese had nearly made it to the hills when they sensed the approaching danger. Taking flight, the first one called to its mate, flying round and round in a panic. The falcon had sighted the shape in the grass and was straining skyward, as if any minute she, too, would take flight, injured wing and all.

Drawing the falcon to him, Dillon tried to calm her, running his hand gently down her back. The geese were some distance away, and he couldn't see what was frightening them and the falcon. Still, he moved in close to a large tree with overhanging branches for protection.

"What is it? What's happening?" he asked the bat. "Is it the Face?"

"No, not the Face," said the bat, listening carefully. "It's another hunter."

The other hunter sprang, leaping out of its hiding place and landing on the injured goose. In those brief seconds Dillon saw the arched body of a cougar and understood the falcon's fear as the large, fierce animal took its prey.

The goose overhead screamed as it flew off and back again, staying safely airborne but reluctant to leave the area and its mate. Dillon tried to remember what his grandmother had said about the ways of cougars. He wondered whether this one would sniff him out and come stalking him and the falcon too. But the big cat took no notice of him. It had picked up its prey and was slowly dragging it back to the hills.

Dillon stayed hidden under the tree, holding the falcon close to him. As he watched the cat, he heard a faint whistling sound somewhere up ahead on the other side of the river. The falcon tensed, her eyes wide and staring into the night. The bat scurried closer to Dillon's neck, and for a moment he remembered stories of bats getting tangled in people's hair. He had always thought that hard to believe since if bats could catch tiny insects at night, how could they not notice something as big as a person's head? Still, he was nervous and wished the bat would move back a bit until he noticed that the small animal was trembling.

The whistling grew louder. At the sound, the cougar picked up speed and had nearly made it to the first hill. Dillon was turning to try to see the bat and ask her if she was all right when the whistling rose suddenly into a sharp, earsplitting screech and the trees further up on the river bent way down as they were hit by a powerful blast of wind.

Dillon went down on his knees, taking the animals with him and becoming as small and hidden as he could. He peered ahead, trying to make out what was happening beyond the screen of leaves the tree provided as protection. A spiraling, dark cloud ripped across the river ahead and rushed with an eerie, high whistling sound out over the plain toward the cougar. The big cat dropped what it held in its mouth and streaked into the hills, disappearing from sight in what seemed to Dillon only seconds.

"It's the Face!" whispered the trembling bat. "Don't move. Don't even breathe!" she added as she clung close to Dillon's ear.

The falcon had become deathly still, watching out over the plain as Dillon held her close with one hand placed gently on her back. Together they watched the dark cloud descend on the body of the goose. Dillon shivered as an unearthly howl of triumph vibrated through the air, rising up from the spiral of smoke and echoing across the valley. The smoky thing plunged and tumbled and rolled around the dead goose. Then it began wandering out in ever-widening circles, searching for something new to engage its morbid interest.

"Quick!" cried the bat. "Follow me."

She darted away from Dillon toward the river, her small wings flapping and gliding silently. Dillon followed close behind, sliding with the falcon down the muddy river bank and crawling in under a mass of overhanging roots. The bank was hollowed out slightly, making a shallow, damp cave where Dillon huddled with his two companions.

For a while he couldn't hear anything. Then a smell of cold, stale ash drifted down on the wind. Around them a low hissing sound came and went, sometimes louder and surprisingly close, and then seeming to be on the other side of the river. He couldn't see anything through the tangled mass of roots, but the bat kept her ears tuned outward, following the path of the Face.

Eventually the hissing grew fainter until it slowly faded into the distance. Around them everything was silent. The night seemed to be holding its breath, waiting and listening. After a while the bat sighed softly in Dillon's ear. He could feel her warm breath on his neck as she spoke.

"I think it's safe now," she whispered.

"Where do you think it went?" asked Dillon, crawling forward to peer out from their hiding place.

"I don't know," said the bat. "Somewhere far out on the plain, or into the mountains. But it didn't find us, at least not this time."

Dillon climbed up the bank, standing still for a moment to look around. The night had shifted back into its starry peace, the murmur of the river sounding pleasantly soothing, as if nothing at all had happened. Dillon's pant legs were streaked with mud, and he felt damp.

"We'll be safer when we get into the mountains," said the bat. "It's rougher going but there are more hiding places."

Moving quickly to shake off the damp chill and

warm up his legs, Dillon threaded his way along the river bank. As they neared the hills, a small, dark speck in the sky grew slowly bigger. The lone goose, who had flown off in terror at the advance of the Face, was circling back, confused and looking for its mate. Its voice called out plaintively, drifting unanswered beneath the dome of silent sky.

Its cry tugged at Dillon. Perhaps he and the goose were alike, he thought. He had lost a close friend too and had been reluctant to leave her behind, and now both he and the goose were left to find their own lonely way through the night.

He felt small and powerless and wished that he were bigger, wished he were bigger than life itself and could turn back time and stop all the miserably sad things from happening. If only he could have reached Carol in time to stop her; if only he had thought to go and rescue the injured goose before the cougar had spotted it. "If only, if only!" he shouted silently in his heart. But he was only one small person in this vast, vast place.

CHAPTER 6

The ground rose upward, climbing the first hill leading into the maze of dark mountains. Any trail that might have been there had long since become overgrown. The bat flew ahead of Dillon, the face of spots on her back leading him around outcroppings of boulders and helping him to avoid ditches that were hidden in thick-growing patches of grass.

Dillon was glad now that the bat had come along. True, she was ugly and creepy with her leathery wings, stubby nose, and huge ears, but she had proved very helpful. If she hadn't come along, he might never have made it this far.

The way became steadily steeper as they moved in and out among tall oak trees rooted precariously on the rocky hillside. Dillon leaned more heavily on the walking stick and the falcon peered ahead of them, her eyes constantly scanning the surrounding landscape. Dillon, too, was alert. The near encounter with the Face had awakened every nerve in his body, and it seemed to him that his sight and hearing had become sharper.

Ahead of him, the bat halted at the base of one of the larger oaks. As he neared her, Dillon could see her shuffling around on the ground.

"What are you doing? Shouldn't we be hurrying?" Dillon asked, watching the bat as she tugged and pulled at a long, flat object.

"Help me," replied the bat, trying to brush away some leaves that partly covered whatever it was she was after. Dillon knelt down and brushed away the leaves. He picked up a large, glossy brown feather as the bat climbed up his sleeve to his shoulder.

"Take it," she said. She flew out from under the tree and Dillon followed her, holding the feather.

"Look up there, near the top of the tree," said the bat.

Leaning back, Dillon looked up at the tall tree silhouetted darkly against the sky. Near the top was what looked like a large mass of closely packed branches.

"It's an eagle's nest," said the bat. "Eagle feathers bring good luck."

Earlier, when he had stood with the wolverine looking out over the valley for the first time, a golden eagle had glided silently past them. It seemed a long time ago to Dillon now, as if many nights had passed instead of just one. He turned the feather over in his hand. Perhaps it had come from the very same bird. If this nest belonged to that same eagle, then it obviously was able to navigate the valley and the mountains safely.

Dillon tucked the feather under his sweatshirt, securing it in the waistband of his jeans. Nodding her satisfaction, the bat took up the lead again as they continued their upward climb.

Eventually they left the hills and came out onto a plateau that dropped steeply downward on one side. Dillon could see clearly back across the star-studded valley to the mountains where they had started out. He stood at the edge of the plateau, wondering if the wolverine were standing somewhere on one of the distant mountains, looking out across to them. For a moment he thought he saw a tiny flicker of light, the opossum's lantern perhaps, across the expanse of valley. Then he blinked, and it was gone.

Turning around, he faced the last obstacle between him and home. The mountains appeared enormous. The plateau butted up against what seemed an unending file of jagged peaks, rising up one behind the other. How was he ever to get through them? His feet ached already, and he doubted if his shoes would survive a long climb over rugged ground.

Behind him came the sound of pebbles scattering down the side of the cliff. The falcon stiffened, and the bat, who had gone off exploring on her own, was flapping hurriedly back to Dillon as he turned again to the edge of the plateau and peered over.

There were some scrubby bushes growing along the top and down the first few yards of the cliff where it was broken in several places by narrow ledges. The edge of the plateau formed an L shape where he stood, and Dillon moved over a few steps so he was standing at the center point where the two sides of the cliff slanted outward. Another scattering of pebbles and small rocks came from below. As he knelt down and leaned farther out for a better look, the falcon fidgeted on his arm, glancing nervously around. The bat plopped suddenly down on Dillon's shoulder, making him jump. Then he saw something move below him.

"I don't think it's a good idea to stay here," said the bat.

Another scrambling sound came from below, and Dillon reached into his pocket for the flashlight.

"Why? It's not the Face. There's no smoke," Dillon said as he ran the beam of light over a ledge beneath them.

The light shone over rocks and clumps of small bushes. The scrambling noise had stopped and everything below had become very still. Then the passing light caught a gleam, and Dillon jerked it back on two large, shining eyes that stared up at him with a mixture of hostility and fear.

"The cougar!" Dillon exclaimed under his breath.

He looked down on the big cat, perched on a ledge so narrow there was barely room to hold her. She had somehow slipped and fallen, and Dillon could see scratches on the side of the cliff where she had tried to climb back up. She had fallen too far to jump back, and the drop was steep with no footholds for climbing. She was trapped.

The falcon was making quick little flapping motions with her uninjured wing, tugging at Dillon's arm.

"I think we should go," said the bat nervously. "Leave well enough alone."

But Dillon did not want to go. Not just yet. He stared down at the cougar, the muscles in his face tightening. Then he picked up a small stone and threw it at the cat. The cat winced and hissed at Dillon, baring large, sharp teeth. He picked up another stone and threw it. This time the cougar growled and lunged up at him, but he was out of reach.

"What are you doing?" screeched the bat, darting off his shoulder and flying frantically overhead.

The falcon was tugging harder at his arm. Dillon ignored them both. His jaw was set hard, and his eyes had narrowed with determination.

"She killed the goose," Dillon said as he threw another stone, hitting the cat in the back.

"But it's not our affair! It's not our affair!" the bat shrieked, flapping in Dillon's face. "Leave well enough alone!"

"She killed the goose!" Dillon shouted back at the bat, bitter, angry tears filling his eyes. She killed the goose, and he wanted to knock her off the cliff, just as he would knock the boys who killed Carol off the cliff if they were stranded there instead of the cat. The cowards had run away, and the cougar had killed the injured goose. He would knock them all off the cliff if he could. He would send them all tumbling away forever.

The bat hovered around Dillon's hand, trying to block him as he picked up another stone.

"It's not our affair!" the bat repeated, her voice shrill and filled with fear.

Dillon tried to brush the bat away but she would not go and kept flapping in front of his hand as he tried to aim at the cougar.

"Listen to me," she begged as Dillon sent the stone hurling through the air. It grazed the bat's wing before landing with a thud on the cat's back. The cat lunged at him again as the bat tumbled to the ground with a small cry.

Dillon stopped as suddenly as he had begun. He watched the bat as she shook herself and tested her wing, afraid that he had injured her. Just then he heard a mewing noise, like a small, frightened cry, coming from a bush a few yards away. Getting up, he went over to the bush. The falcon had stopped tugging at his arm but had drawn away from him, sitting rigidly motionless and staring at him with wide, round eyes.

Carefully he drew aside the branches and saw a small cougar cub huddled under the bush, trembling. It hissed at him, trying to back away. Dillon returned to the edge of the cliff and shone the light on the cat. She hissed and growled as he ran the light over her, taking in what he hadn't noticed before; she was a mother.

Not only did she have milk, but she was thin, and he could see the faint outline of her ribs. She was a mother, and she was hungry, and he had been throwing stones at her, trying to knock her to her death, and all because she had been trying to feed herself and her cub by hunting the goose.

Dillon sat slowly down, bending his head and covering his face with his hand. It was too much. In a night full of so many hard things, he thought, this was just too much. He pounded his fist on the ground, angry at himself for being stupidly cruel and at the same time feeling an immeasurable sadness for all the unending misery in the world. He was glad Carol wasn't there to see how he had treated the cat. And his grandmother, too. They wouldn't have liked it. Maybe they would have understood, though, how hard it was for him to be lost in this place by himself.

Pained sobs broke from his throat and tears streamed down his face. The bat crawled slowly across the ground to him. The stone had only grazed her, causing no serious injury. Cautiously she approached. When the crying subsided, she spoke softly in his ear.

"Please, let's go," she said. "It's not much farther now, really."

Dillon took the bat in his hand, holding her so he could see her huge ears and tiny face.

"Are you all right?" he asked. "Can you fly?"

"Yes. The stone only nicked me," she replied.

He set the bat on his shoulder and wiped his face on his sleeve. Then he ran his hand gently down the falcon's back and over her injured wing. She fluffed her feathers and blinked at him.

"Okay," said Dillon. "But first there's something I have to do," he added, getting to his feet.

"What?" asked the bat as Dillon headed for an isolated cluster of trees. Dillon did not answer. He searched the ground until he found a very large, thick branch that had broken off from a tree. Setting his walking stick down, he pulled on the branch with both hands. The falcon flapped her good wing in an effort to help as he slowly dragged the branch over to the cliff.

"What are you doing?" asked the bat again.

"You'll see," said Dillon between breaths.

The cougar growled and hissed and swatted at him as he carefully lowered the branch down toward her. Lodging it securely between some rocks, he let his end drop against the top of the cliff. Then he backed away quickly and returned to the stand of trees, where he recovered his walking stick and waited.

He didn't have long to wait. The cat's head soon appeared as she climbed up the branch to safety. She stood looking around only a moment before darting to the bush where her cub lay hidden. Over the distance between them Dillon could hear a faint mewing and saw the cub scramble out to its mother.

While he watched, Dillon heard another sound: a distant, low whistling. Pricking up her ears, the cougar stiffened. The bat and falcon heard it, too, and they all strained to tell the direction it was coming from. For a moment nothing moved. Then the cat and her cub suddenly broke across the plateau for the cover of the mountains, and Dillon and his companions turned and fled toward the first towering, rocky peak just as the low whistling grew into a shriek, and the spiraling shroud of ghostly smoke lunged up over the edge of the cliff and came speeding toward them.

CHAPTER 7

*A*bove the pounding of his heart Dillon could hear the howling cry of the Face as it pursued them into the mountains. The falcon was flapping furiously, pulling him along as he scrambled with one hand over fallen rocks, trying to keep track of the flying bat as she turned deftly in and out among huge boulders. There were few trees here; the land was strangely barren, cut with cliffs and crevices and strewn with boulders.

Dillon thought he heard the howling falter, as if the Face had paused in its pursuit. Perhaps it couldn't decide which to go after—the cats or them. They had gone in different directions and it couldn't catch them all, Dillon thought. He hoped it wouldn't catch any of them.

As he inched around a rock face with only a skinny

ledge for footing, he heard the howling pick up again. There was no mistaking the direction it had taken this time; it grew louder as the Face sought them out among the rocks. Dillon jumped across a narrow crevice to a wider foothold and nearly slipped. A scattering of stones and dirt clattered down the mountain. Following the bat, he slid in between two boulders and climbed to more solid ground.

The white spots on the bat's back bobbed up and down as she led him across a small clearing and into one of the few stands of trees in the bleak landscape. The howling had grown so loud it pierced Dillon's ears, and he could smell the acrid fumes of the Face's shroud as it surged up the mountainside behind them. They darted in under the trees which stood at the base of another cliff. The bat flew frantically back and forth, looking for something.

"Here!" she cried, her voice almost lost in the howling roar.

Dillon followed her into a crack in the cliff barely wide enough for him and the falcon to squeeze into. He moved back until it was too narrow for him to go any further and turned to face the opening. Trees hid the entrance to their refuge, and Dillon watched as the branches were whipped around in a fury. The Face was looking for them, rushing in and out among the rocks and trees.

"Get down!" cried the bat as she grabbed onto his shoulder.

Dillon crouched down in the narrow space, trying

not to choke on the reek of ash and decay that had become unbearably strong. He raised his head slowly and looked up at the opening. A dense cloud of smoke obliterated the swaying trees, and as he watched, he saw two huge, hollow eyes loom up out of the murk. The lifeless eyes searched the shadows. Dillon held his breath and shut his eyes, wishing he was as small and dark as the bat. He could feel the eagle feather against his skin beneath the torn and dirty sweatshirt and imagined himself a hawk, soaring higher and higher, away from danger.

The howling continued for what seemed an eternity. The Face screamed and whirled about along the cliff wall and among the boulders and crags. It couldn't find Dillon and his companions, concealed as they were in the dark shadow of the fissure. Finally it moved farther away, still searching and howling. The stale odor of cold ash lingered long after Dillon could no longer hear the Face's awful shrieking.

Starlight filtered through the branches as Dillon crawled to the opening. The ground was littered with broken branches, as though a hurricane had struck the mountainside. Dillon moved cautiously out into the open and glanced around.

"I thought you said we'd be safer in the mountains," he whispered to the bat. He was shivering, not from the cold but from the memory of the empty eyes that had peered into their hiding place, looking for them.

"There are more hiding places here than on the

plain," replied the bat. "We would have been safer if you hadn't let the Face know where we were."

"I what?" asked Dillon, turning his head to stare at the bat on his shoulder.

The bat sighed. "I warned you about the flashlight," she said. "When you beamed it on the cougar you sent a signal out across the valley. Anyone could have seen it."

Dillon frowned and ran his hand through his hair, pulling it out of his face.

"I tried to stop you," continued the bat, "but you wouldn't listen. You were too intent on knocking the cat to her death. That alone, even without the flashlight, would have been enough to attract the Face. It can scent death from miles away."

Dillon stared down at his shoes. It was not pleasant to realize that by his own actions he had brought them all within the grasp of the Face.

"It won't happen again," he said, looking up at the bat.

"No, I don't think it will," she said thoughtfully, agreeing with him.

Dillon glanced around at the moonlit peaks still to be crossed. The toe on one of his shoes was ripped open and the sole on the other one had come loose in back. It flapped a little when he walked.

"There's a cave up ahead that leads deep into the mountains," said the bat. "It stretches for miles. I think we should take it so we can travel unseen."

The idea didn't appeal to Dillon. Caves were dark, airless places where a person could get lost.

"Have you been in the cave before?" he asked the bat.

"Oh, yes," said the little animal. "I've been in all the caves. I know them like the back of my wing."

The falcon was leaning forward on Dillon's arm, straining toward the peaks ahead. Every so often she'd glance up at the sky and make nervous, fluttering motions with her wing.

"Let's go," said Dillon, noting the falcon's impatience. Though the thought of walking, or maybe even crawling, through miles of caves was not very appealing, it was even less appealing to contemplate being hunted again by the Face.

"Where's the cave?" Dillon asked the bat.

"Beyond the next rise," she said. "If we hurry we might make it safely inside before we're spotted again," she added, flapping alongside Dillon.

The bat led Dillon around a large crag and up a steep, narrow trail. The moon had grown larger and moved lower in the sky. It crowned the top of a peak ahead of them and glowed with a golden brilliance. Dillon's feet sent pebbles and dirt tumbling into the darkness below, and he gripped at whatever hold he could find to steady himself. At the top of the trail was a ledge that slanted downwards a few feet to a small opening in the wall of rock.

"Is that the cave?" asked Dillon, pointing at the opening. It was hardly big enough for him; he would have to stoop to get through it.

"Yes, but it's bigger inside," said the bat. "You'll see. Come on."

The bat flitted into the cave, and Dillon bent down to follow, using the walking stick to feel out the way ahead. It was pitch black inside. He fumbled in his pocket for the flashlight and turned it on.

The small opening led into a cavern that stretched back into the mountain. With relief, Dillon stood up straight. He didn't care for crawling. He shone the light around at the rocky walls.

"Is it this high all the way?" he asked the bat.

"Well, most of it is," said the bat. "There are a few small places, but you'll fit."

Dillon returned to the opening and, stooping down, went back outside. He knew he was going to have to go down into the mountain, but he wanted one last look at the moon before doing so. Across from the cave and down a ways was another barren plateau, separated from him by a deep ravine. He thought he could see something moving out on the plateau but it was too far for him to make out clearly.

"What's that over there?" he called to the bat. "Something's moving out there."

Joining him at the mouth of the cave, the bat listened carefully. How strange to be able to see with your ears, thought Dillon as he watched the bat. Not a bad idea for getting around in the dark, though. He touched his own ears and for a moment wondered what it would be like to listen to things the way the bat did.

"It's the cougar and her cub," said the bat finally.

Good, thought Dillon. They had managed to escape the Face. He stroked the falcon's back as the wind tousled his hair and ruffled her feathers. Then the bat motioned to a spot further down. In the distance the whirling column of smoke was twisting its way up the side of the ravine.

"It's coming," said the bat. "We'd better get inside before it spots us."

Dillon hesitated, watching the dark blur of the cats running across the plateau, which was separated from the surrounding mountains by encircling gullies and ravines. Having climbed that far, there was no place left for the animals to go except back down the way they'd come up, and that route was blocked by the Face. Remembering the awful, lifeless eyes, Dillon worried that the cats would be cornered, stranded on open ground with no place to hide.

"If the Face followed us into the mountain, would we be trapped?" asked Dillon.

"Not if we could reach the river and make it to the other side before it found us," answered the bat. "But let's not take any chances," she added, inching back into the cave.

"What river?" asked Dillon, surprised at the idea of a river in a mountain.

"The underground river, of course," said the bat, coming to a halt and looking up at Dillon. "Don't you know anything about caves?"

"No, not really," said Dillon, chewing on his lower lip while he thought hard about something. The Face was gaining ground, slipping over the rocky surfaces and around jutting boulders.

"Let's go," said the bat.

"No. I mean, not yet," said Dillon, still thinking. "If we had a head start, do you think there's a chance we could outrun the Face and make it to the river?" he asked.

"Perhaps," replied the bat slowly. "If we had a good enough head start. Can you swim?" she asked.

"Yes," said Dillon.

The bat climbed up Dillon's sleeve and scrutinized his face as he followed the smoky shroud's advance up to the plateau. She had an idea of what Dillon was up to, and there was at least some chance it might work. The bat sighed; she'd taken on more than she had anticipated when she'd first offered to help him. Maybe he wasn't quite so young after all.

The cougar and cub had reached the far side of the plateau and were circling back, looking for a way down. Drawing the falcon in close to him, Dillon knelt down, took a long, deep breath and raised the flashlight. He rolled up onto his toes and tightened his muscles, ready to sprint back into the cave. The falcon tensed for flight as the Face gained the top of the ravine and whipped out over the plateau. Dillon aimed the light across the ravine and flicked it rapidly on and off, on and off.

Like a signal, the blinking light startled the Face. The swirling mass of smoke paused and hung spinning in the air, hiding the deathly mask within. Then it turned and dipped and spun and came rushing toward them.

Dillon, too, spun around and dove into the mouth of the cave. No point in not using the flashlight now, he thought. It gave enough light to see the bat's bobbing white spots as she flew frantically ahead of him. Under his shirt he could feel the eagle feather rubbing against him as he ran. The falcon half flew, half pulled on his arm as they plunged deep into the mountain.

CHAPTER 8

Twisting downward, the cave narrowed. There was still plenty of room for Dillon to run upright, and the ripped sole on his shoe flapped over the stone floor as they tunneled farther and farther away from the night outside. Dillon couldn't hear anything behind them yet, so he figured they must have gotten a good head start. The Face would have to cross the ravine before it could reach the cave. His heart was pounding, though only partly from fear. It was also strangely exhilarating to think that he might possibly trick the Face out of getting any of its quarry—neither him nor the cats.

As they rounded a bend, Dillon came to a quick stop where the cave suddenly ended. There was a thick rock wall in front of him, and he couldn't see the bat.

"Down here" came the bat's voice from the vicinity

of Dillon's knees. He bent down to a very narrow opening and saw that the bat was already inside.

"Come on," she said. "You'll fit. It's not very far.
Really."

Dillon didn't see how he and the falcon could possibly fit. "Isn't there another way?" he asked the bat
anxiously.

"No," came her voice from the darkness. "Lie down
on your back and scoot in. It isn't far, I promise."

Lying down on his back, Dillon pushed himself
head-first into the opening with his feet. The narrow
walls were unbearably close, and he fought against the
panic that rose at the idea of getting stuck and maybe
suffocating. But the bat was right; it wasn't very far.
After a few yards the tunnel ended in a cavern.

Their shadows danced in gigantic silhouettes over
the walls as they darted across the cavern to another
small opening. This time Dillon scooted through without any prompting from the bat. He was straining his
ears to catch the slightest sound of the Face behind
them. He felt like he had been running and hiding and
running for eons. What if he got stuck in this place, the
place with no name? What kind of place was it, anyway?
A dream? Eternity? What if he was stuck in eternity,
running and running with no end?

Have to stop thinking wild things, Dillon told himself. There was certainly no turning back now. He'd just
have to keep going until they reached the underground river. He hoped the bat was right about the
Face being unable to follow them beyond it.

They had come out of the second tunnel and were

climbing down a ledge, Dillon hugging the wall on one side to keep from looking over the other side where the floor dropped down into pitch-black nothingness. Because of the steep descent and rough ground, he moved slower, using the flashlight to pick out the loose stones and taking care not to trip and risk going over the edge.

"Why can't the Face get us if we cross the river?" he asked the bat, remembering that the Face had no problem crossing a river when it snatched away the cougar's kill.

"Because it doesn't like water," said the bat.

This didn't make much sense to Dillon. "But rivers are water," he pointed out. "The Face crossed the river on the plain."

"Yes," said the bat between breaths. She was a small animal and was beginning to tire. "It crossed over the river, not under it," she went on.

Dillon stopped short.

"We're going under the river?" he asked wide-eyed.

"Sort of," said the bat. "In a manner of speaking, that is."

Dillon looked at the falcon, wondering if she could swim. And what about the bat, he thought? He'd never heard of bats swimming.

"Can you swim under water?" he asked her.

"Oh hurry, please," said the bat, pausing to listen. "Can you hear that?" she asked. Dillon listened too. Somewhere far behind them he heard a faint, low hissing.

"Come on. There's no time to waste," said the bat.

"And we don't have to swim under the river; we can walk under it." With this, she sped off ahead of a bewildered Dillon, beckoning for him to follow.

The bat darted into a tunnel and led them to a place where the cave forked, choosing another tunnel that twisted down and around to yet another branching. In this way they went on through a maze of turns and tunnels, all the while the hissing behind them growing louder.

Dillon thought they must be very far below the mountains by now and wondered how much further it could be when they turned down another passage and entered a large, cavernous room. The flashlight was barely strong enough to pierce the gloomy shadows above and around him. He could make out dim openings in the rock wall, some high above his head, where many passages led into and out of the cavern.

The bat headed for an opening on the far side with Dillon following close behind. As they approached it he could see that by stooping he could manage to get through. He was bending down to enter when a gust of fetid air burst into the cavern. Dillon turned quickly to glance behind him. From a dark hole high in a wall a dense stream of smoke was pouring down. Suddenly a loud howl shook the cavern as the Face appeared in the opening and turned its lightless, empty eyes on Dillon.

Dillon fled into the hole behind the bat, scraping his back on the stone roof of the tunnel. Behind him he could hear the frenzied whistling of the Face while ahead of him he picked up another sound. The river, he thought, it must be the river. In a moment the sound of rushing water was unmistakable as the tunnel ended above the slanting, gravel shore of the underground river.

CHAPTER 9

illon and the falcon slid down the bank to the water's edge. It ran through a long, low room. Little streams joined it, trickling down over the walls and spilling into the river. Further along on the opposite bank, there was a shallow grotto where a larger stream tumbled from a high opening and cascaded down in a waterfall to a creek that merged with the river. The sound of rushing water was everywhere.

The bat was at Dillon's ear. "Cross the river to the waterfall," she shouted. "Behind it there's safety. The Face can't follow us there."

With the sound of the Face so close behind them, Dillon plunged into the river. The water came up to his knees and was shockingly cold. His feet slipped between fist-sized rocks as he angled across the river, heading downstream. The bat flew in front of him and the current pushed from behind. As the water rose to chest level he had only seconds to wonder how in the world he was going to swim with the falcon on his arm when, with a dreadful shriek and a sudden blast of air, the Face rushed out of the tunnel.

Dillon clamped the thin flashlight between his teeth and swam. He held the walking stick like a bar out in front of him as the falcon flapped and pulled and he kicked with all his strength. Together they pushed on toward the opposite bank. Howling, the Face tumbled and rolled above the surface of the water. Dillon coughed and choked and tried desperately to keep his burning eyes open as the smoke spread out across the river. Beneath the uproar, he heard the tiny voice of the bat close to his ear.

"Straight ahead," she cried. "Keep going!"

The falcon's flapping was becoming weak and fitful. Dillon thought that at any moment he would sink beneath the surface, choking and gasping for air. Through the howling came the sound of the waterfall drawing closer. With a surge of strength, he pushed ahead and his outstretched hand hit against rock. His feet touched bottom, and he pulled himself up out of the river, dragging himself onto the bank.

Gripping the flashlight in his hand, Dillon stumbled and slipped over the rocks to the creek fed by the waterfall. Barely able to breathe and with eyes shut tight against the stinging, swirling smoke, he groped his way blindly along the narrow bank. Shutting out all thought except the will to keep moving, his hands followed the rock wall toward the sound of falling water. The falcon shuddered and gasped on his arm, and he felt an oppressive weight pushing him down.

He was on his knees, scraping his knuckles and hands as he crawled slowly forward. Suddenly he felt a touch of spray on his cheek. Then a puff of moist air penetrated the suffocating smoke, and he could hear the waterfall directly in front of him. Another gust of cool, wet air and Dillon gulped, opening his eyes to two thin slits.

The mist from the falling water was scattering the Face's dense shroud. Dillon gasped for air and heaved himself to his feet. Safety lay within arm's reach on the other side of the waterfall. The bat was right; the Face would not be able to follow them through the cascading shield of water. Already the mist was pushing it back.

Then Dillon's heart jumped. He spun around, shining the flashlight over the walls and along the creek bank. Where was the bat? He hadn't noticed when her voice went silent. Panic tightened his throat as he took a few cautious steps back along the bank, searching for the bat. The Face had retreated from the spray and mist to the mouth of the creek and hung there, spinning in the air and howling.

The flashlight played over a small brown body, almost indistinguishable from the rocks, lying along the bank between Dillon and the Face. Water lapped against the bat's body, threatening to pull it down into the creek. Dillon stood very still, looking from the bat to the Face. Little tentacles of smoke whipped out from the Face's shroud and danced around the bat.

What had the wolverine said? It seemed so very long ago. He tried desperately to remember what he had not been able to understand at the time. Something about the Face. The Face has no face at all? That was it. "Fear can paint a face on anything," the wolverine had said.

The falcon shook herself, sending a spray of water into the air. Dillon stepped into the stream, standing ankle-deep in the cool, rushing water, still within the protective shroud of mist. He looked at the bat, hoping she was still alive. He thought he saw her move, but maybe it was only the water tugging at her. Then he looked up at the looming mask of the Face. No, he thought, gritting his teeth. No. I'm not leaving without her.

He took a step toward the bat. The Face rose up several feet higher in the air and pierced the cavern with a deafening shriek. Dillon took another step and the Face spun and shrieked again, reaching out with smoky arms towards the bat.

"No!" yelled Dillon, kicking a spray of water toward the Face. "No!" he yelled again, running forward.

The Face whirled and dived at Dillon, who had left the waterfall behind as he ran shouting down the creek until he stood between the bat and the Face. His eyes stung from the smoke as he kicked a huge spray of water at the advancing Face. The Face drew back momentarily just as a long cry pierced the cavern, not the cry of the Face but a sound Dillon had never heard before. The falcon had drawn herself up on his arm and spread both her wings, calling in a long, cascading cry that echoed through the cavern for all the earth to hear.

Without thinking, Dillon threw back his head and yelled defiantly, his own voice bouncing off the walls and rolling out across the water. He ran at the Face, shouting and kicking water. The Face shrunk back and drew in its shroud. Then it lunged at him again, shrieking and whirling with its lifeless eyes only a few feet from Dillon's own.

Dillon shouted and lunged back, striking out at the awful eyes. His arm passed right through the mask. The Face drew back, and Dillon pulled himself up as tall as he could and shouted in triumph, drowning the Face's screeching with his own voice as it retreated within its diminishing shroud. For the moment at least, Dillon felt he was truly larger than life itself. Shouting and kicking and splashing, he pushed the Face back out over the river.

The Face's shrieking became fainter and the deathly shroud began to shrivel into thin threads of smoke. Soon only a few gray wisps remained as the last of the Face slunk back into the mountain, slipping into whatever cracks and holes it could find. Dillon stood watching and listening until all he could hear was the sound of water rushing down and over rocks.

He made his way back to the bat. She didn't move

when he picked her up, but he could feel her heart beating. Gently, he tucked the small, wet body under his T-shirt and stood up.

He gazed at the falcon, who stared back at him with her sharp gaze. How long ago it seemed that he had first seen those eyes, sparkling like stars in the gathering gloom of that faraway hillside. How very long ago everything seemed. He turned slowly and listened to the splashing of his own feet as he walked through the shallow water to the falls.

CHAPTER 10

In the recessed shelter behind the waterfall, Dillon sat down against the wall. A cool draft entered the area from one of two passageways that led off on either side from where he sat. He was back far enough from the falling water to be clear of its spray. Setting the flashlight down on the dry ground in front of him, he leaned back and closed his eyes.

The falcon had shaken the water from her feathers and sat quietly, perched on his arm. He put his hand over the lump in his shirt and felt the little bat stir underneath. When he brought her out she coughed and spat water, then blinked at him silently. He reached under his shirt and felt the eagle feather still securely in place, though soaked like the rest of him. For a while all three quietly recovered their strength, sitting in the small halo of light cast by the flashlight.

"I almost thought we wouldn't make it," said the bat at last, speaking softly. "Certainly I wouldn't have made it if you hadn't turned back for me," she added, shaking a drop of water from her nose.

"You don't think I would have left you behind with the Face, do you?" he asked slowly, watching the bat shake another drop from her ear.

"No." The bat seemed to smile. "You would never have done that."

Dillon glanced at the passages on either side of them. The Face was gone. At least, he was pretty sure it was gone. There probably wasn't much chance of it showing up again. Even if it did, he figured he could howl as fiercely as any phantom. All the same, he was not inclined to linger, not after what they'd just been through and not while they were still in a sunless cave under the mountains.

He pulled himself slowly to his feet. He was scratched and dirty, wet and shivering. The sooner they got out of there the better, he thought.

"Which way do we go?" he asked.

"You have to go that way," said the bat, motioning to one of the passageways. "It'll take you up and out of the mountains on the far side from the valley."

"Aren't you coming, too?" asked Dillon.

"No, I'm going back," she said. "The others will be waiting for me." She looked up at him with her small, dark eyes. "The rest of the way is easy now. You'll be all right."

Dillon wasn't really worried about himself. He didn't see how anything could be much worse than what he'd already been through. It was just that he'd become so used to the bat's company that he hadn't thought about her leaving.

"What about you?" he asked. "Will you be all right going back by yourself?"

The bat almost smiled. "I'm small and hard to see when I'm traveling alone," she answered.

Dillon wiped his face on his sleeve. He picked up the flashlight, amazed that it was still working. The falcon stretched each leg in turn and shook some water from her tail as he leaned on the walking stick. He looked at the bat on his shoulder. She'd been a great help to him, and he didn't know what to say to her.

"Next time I'm out at night, I'll look for you," he said finally.

The bat nodded. "Yes. Perhaps we'll meet again," she said, but Dillon could tell she didn't really think so. "The next time you're out at night, I don't think you'll be quite so lost," she said, flitting around above him and shaking the last drops of water from her wings. Then she darted to the beginning of the passage she would take back through the mountains.

"Just follow that tunnel all the way out," she said, motioning to the one behind him. "It will take you home," she called as she flew off in the other direction, the white spots on her back bobbing into the darkness.

Dillon watched her go before turning and starting slowly up the tunnel that would lead him out of the mountains. His wet hair hung in his face, and his clothes clung to him. He stopped to push the hair from his eyes and then went on, lighting the way with the skinny beam of the flashlight. Perched calmly on his arm, the falcon sat fluffed and quiet, watching ahead as the light pushed aside the shadows, only to have them close up again behind them.

Upwards they climbed, Dillon's shoe flapping softly in the otherwise silent tunnel. They kept a steady pace, though Dillon's shoulders slumped a bit, and he kept reaching up to brush wet strands of hair from his tired eyes.

It was a little lonely without the bat, he thought. She certainly knew her way around in the dark and wasn't afraid of caves or anything else, except the Face. He glanced around at the silent walls. He hoped there were no other phantoms to be dealt with because he was really very tired. All he wanted was to get home. His parents must be terribly worried, and Carol and Mary Jane were still alone. He quickened his pace as much as his aching legs would allow.

Smaller passages branched off from the tunnel, but Dillon unerringly kept to the main route, following the draft of cool air that blew down from some place far ahead. Eventually the black shadows in front of him turned to dark gray and slowly began to lighten as he approached a bend in the tunnel. Reaching it, he felt a rush of cool air and saw a faint glimmer of daylight ahead. A few more steps took him around another turn, and suddenly he found himself standing in a shallow cave facing a wide opening. He blinked at the sunlight streaking into the cave.

Beyond the opening, Dillon could see the pointed, green peaks of countless trees across which the sun was slowly rising like a fiery crimson disk on the distant red horizon. He watched as bands of red and orange and pink spread out across the dawn sky, chasing away the dark blues and grays of night. Through all his aching tiredness, a slow smile spread across Dillon's face. He looked at the falcon and his smile widened. They had made it. Together they had found their way through the strange and seemingly endless night.

He stood at the mouth of the cave and looked down the long hillside to a thin ribbon of familiar highway in the distance. With a jump he left the cave behind, running across a small rockfall and pushing through bushes until he came to a stream. An old fallen tree lay along the bank, and Dillon sat down, leaning his back against it. He took off his shoes and dipped his sore feet into the cool water.

The autumn sun still held some of its summer warmth, and Dillon closed his eyes as it filtered through the trees and ran over his legs and arms and up over his head. The chill of the night began to fade as he leaned over the water in the early morning sunshine, cupping his hand to drink and splashing the dust and dirt from his face. He nearly dunked his whole head in the stream, so that rivulets of water ran down from his hair.

The falcon drank, too. She dipped her head into the water and sent a shower of drops over her back. Shaking her feathers, she dipped and showered again.

Dillon took handfuls of water and gently wiped away the dirt and dried blood from her injured wing. It didn't look quite so bad when it was cleaned up, he thought. Maybe it would heal all right, and she would be able to fly again.

Leaning back, Dillon rested his head against the log. An overgrown dirt track led around the fallen tree, and Dillon could see where the track took up again on the other side of the stream. He would follow that down, he thought. It was bound to come out near the highway below. But first he would rest. He was exhausted from the journey. He would rest and then follow the track, and soon he would be home. Thinking this, he closed his eyes.

Ever since Dillon had found the falcon, she had clung to him, her feet wrapped firmly around his arm. Quietly now, she left him and climbed onto the fallen tree. She sat above him, silent and alert, turning to follow the slightest movement in the surrounding woods. Dillon didn't know this, though. His breathing had become soft and regular, and he was very deeply asleep.

CHAPTER 11

Dillon woke up warm and dry, his head resting on a soft pillow. He gazed around at the walls of the room for a few moments before he recognized them. The glass-fronted cabinet near the window had once belonged to his grandfather, and the books and model airplanes on the shelves inside were his own. The blanket was his, too, and the clothes over the chair and the rug on the floor. He was home, in his own room.

He was surprised at this though not sure why he should be. He tried hard to remember something but the thought escaped him, so he stared at the window instead, blinking in the bright sunlight. There were a few rocks on the sill and a turtle shell and something else that hadn't been there before.

Getting up and going over to the window, Dillon

feather. He held it up, and the sun ... it to a golden brown. The events of the night flooded back as he turned the eagle feather over in the ... The ... and the bat, Carol and the ... and the ... came rushing back, and he sat down on the bed wondering if any of it was true. It ... all been a dream.

He heard the back door slam downstairs. Quietly he left ... and went along the hall to the head of the stairs. From the kitchen below, he could hear his parents' ... speaking low so as not to waken him. He crept halfway down the stairs until their words were clearer.

"I don't understand how he found that old cart track," his father was saying. "Nobody's used that track since Mother was a young girl. She used to go up there berry picking."

"Let's be thankful he did," said his mother, "or he might still be wandering around up there lost."

"That bird's the strangest thing, though," his father continued. "Nobody can figure out what it was doing there. The sheriff said he could have sworn it was watching over Dillon. And the belt and sock wrapped around his wrist, all ripped up? What was that for? You know he's always been afraid of large birds."

The falcon! Was she all right, Dillon wondered? And how did they know he was afraid of birds? He'd never told anyone that. He leaned over the railing and listened. His mother was running water at the sink. When she was done he heard her speaking again.

"Well, we can ask him about that when he wakes up," she said. "They're holding the memorial service for Carol the day after tomorrow," she went on. "What an awful thing to happen. I still can't believe that lively young girl is gone."

Dillon crept back to his room. So they knew everything. They'd found Carol and Mary Jane. Mary Jane? He went over to the window and looked out. There she was, asleep in her favorite spot under an apple tree. He sat down heavily on his bed. At least he didn't have to break the news about the shooting himself.

He'd never been to a memorial service before. He wondered if it'd be terribly sad and if he'd have to speak to Carol's parents. He didn't know what he'd say. That she loved hawks? They knew that already. That he missed her? He was sure they knew all too well about missing her. That he was sorry he'd been unable to stop her from charging up the hill? He wondered if they'd blame him. He guessed they knew Carol well enough to know that she'd do anything, even something crazy, to save a bird.

And the bird was safe; the sheriff had seen it. It wasn't a dream. He got up from the bed and dressed quickly, tucking the eagle feather under his shirt. He needed to ask his parents a few questions.

When he entered the kitchen, both his parents got up and hugged him in turn. His mother ran her hand through his hair.

"You've got a bruise on your head," she said. "How do you feel? Does your head hurt?"

"No, it doesn't hurt," said Dillon. "I'm okay, really."

"Well, come on and have something to eat," said his father.

They all sat down at the table. Dillon rested his hands in his lap and looked from one parent to the other as they passed him toast and jam and sausage.

"I'll fix you some eggs," said his mother, getting up.

"No, I'm not that hungry. Really. This is fine," Dillon said, drawing the plate of food closer to him. He sat for a while staring at the plate, not touching anything. Then he looked up at the two anxious faces watching him.

"What happened to the bird?" he asked.

"That's what we'd like to know," said his father.

"I mean, did you see her?" Dillon asked.

"No, but the sheriff saw her," his mother said. "When he found you, he said you were curled up fast asleep and a full-grown falcon was perched on a log above your head. It looked like it was watching over you, just like some guardian angel, he said."

Dillon looked down at his hands. He felt under his shirt for the eagle feather then looked back up at his mother.

"But what's happened to her?" he asked. "Where is she?"

"The sheriff said she flew away when he approached," his mother said. "She didn't fly too well, he said. He thought she might have been shot. Looked like one of her wings was injured. But she flew just the same and made it up high enough in a tree to be out of his reach."

Dillon sighed with relief. If she could fly even a little bit, maybe she would be okay after all.

His father coughed.

"Carol's parents are planning to take food up to the bird until it recovers its strength. They'll wait and see if it flies well enough when the wing heals," his father said, giving Dillon a curious, questioning look. Dillon looked down at his plate.

"We know what happened to Carol," his father went on. "One of the boys involved in the shooting got home last night all upset and told what happened. He said they'd been shooting at a bird in a tree and it was all an accident." His father paused. Dillon continued staring down at his plate.

"It was pretty late by the time we got up there," his mother said. "We found Carol and Mary Jane but we couldn't find you."

"I got lost, I guess," Dillon said. "Missed the logging road somehow." He picked up his fork and played absently with the sausages on his plate.

"We're very sorry about Carol," said his mother. "We liked her very much. We'll all miss her." She reached over to brush the hair out of Dillon's eyes and added with a sad smile, "I remember the time she came rushing through the door, looking for you with a field mouse in her pocket she'd just saved from a cat."

Dillon smiled a sad smile, too, remembering how his mother had jumped at the sight of the mouse. He had jumped too, but he didn't think anyone had noticed.

"We'll all miss her," said his father quietly. "It was a

terrible thing to have happened. She was a bright, very nice girl."

"Yes, I know," said Dillon softly, still looking down at his plate. He shifted in his seat and looked up at his parents. "She liked bats, you know," he said.

"I think she liked just about everything that crawls, swims, or flies," said his mother, smiling.

Getting up, his father carried his plate over to the sink. He stayed staring out the window a while before returning to sit back down at the table.

"Carol's parents said you two were out looking for a falcon's nest. Was the falcon the sheriff saw the same bird the boys were shooting at?" his father asked.

"Yes," said Dillon.

His parents looked at each other and then back at Dillon.

"How did it get there?" his mother asked.

"I carried it," said Dillon.

His father drew in a deep breath and let it out slowly. "You carried that bird all the way down that old cart track, in the dark, by yourself?" he asked slowly. "It's not that I don't believe you," he went on quickly. "It's just that I've never heard anything like it. That trail's a long way around and hard to find, it's so overgrown."

Dillon didn't want to tell them about the bat and the wolverine, and the strange little opossum with the tiny lantern, or the wide valley with its golden moon and falling stars. And he couldn't tell them about the Face with its lifeless, hollow eyes. It all felt very real to him, but he was sure they wouldn't understand. They'd think it was only a dream.

His father was speaking again.

"Carrying that bird all that way. I thought you didn't like birds," he was saying.

"I had to take her," Dillon answered, clearing his throat. "She was hurt and couldn't fly at all when I found her. If I'd left her she might have died."

"You did the right thing," his mother said. "We were awfully worried about you, though. Your father and I, the sheriff and others, were out looking for you all night. We're glad you're home." She gave him another hug as she got up to pour more coffee.

Dillon took a bite of sausage. He spread some jam on a piece of toast and ate that too. Both his parents looked pretty tired, so he thought he wouldn't bother them with any more questions just then. He did want to ask Carol's parents if he could go with them when they went to leave food for the falcon. And he thought he might try to find the cave he had come out of after the long journey underground. Perhaps the whole night was only a dream, but if dreams were also shadows of something real, then the cave might be there some-where, waiting for him to find it.

His father pushed back his chair. "I guess I'll go try to get some sleep," he said, getting up. He reached across the table and ruffled Dillon's hair. "Sure were glad to see you this morning, even if you were sound asleep. We tried to wake you up, but you just mumbled something about rivers and bats and went back to

sleep." He smiled at Dillon as he stretched his back and
yawned.

"I wonder if anyone's heard anything about the
other boy yet," his mother said.

"Which boy?" asked Dillon.

"The one who did the shooting," she said. "He
never went home last night. Took the family pickup
and drove up into the hills."

"He's probably pretty shaken up," said his father, as
he cleared the breakfast dishes off the table. "Everyone
knows the shooting was an accident, but those boys
shouldn't have been out hunting at all. Let's hope the
boy comes home when he calms down and thinks
reasonably."

Yawning again, his father went off to get some
sleep. Dillon helped his mother finish cleaning up,
then went out to the garage. Mary Jane wandered in
the open door and came up to him, wagging her tail.
He scratched her behind the ears and patted her back.
Then he knelt down and hugged her.

"Good old girl," he whispered in her ear. "You
stayed with Carol just like I told you." The dog licked
his face and whipped her tail around in circles.

A workbench sat beneath a dusty, cobwebbed window in the back of the garage. Pieces of assorted
watches were strewn over the top of it. Mary Jane
curled up at Dillon's feet as he sat down on a stool,
pushing the bits around with his finger. He wondered
if the truck he had heard just before he and the falcon
had fled into the woods had been the other boy,

the one who did the shooting. Maybe he had become lost too.

He didn't think he really cared all that much what happened to the boy. He never wanted to see him again, accident or no accident. But if the boy had wandered high into the mountains and come across the wolverine, would the wolverine have spoken to him? The old animal had said that sometimes people wander in lost and afraid, and sometimes they find their way home again, thinking it was all just a dream. Did everyone find their way home again, Dillon wondered? He hoped the boy had the sense to listen to the wolverine.

Taking a pair of tweezers, he picked up a tiny hour hand and inserted it into a watch face. He thought about searching for the cave and wondered if any bats lived in it. He supposed he could find out by setting up a pre-dawn watch to see if any came back before sunrise to roost in the dark, stony interior.

Carol would have liked that. What would she have said, he wondered, if she'd seen him with the tiny bat on his shoulder and the falcon on his arm? She probably would have laughed at the sight of him calmly adorned with animals that had once made him cringe. The thought made him smile. He wished he could tell her about it. Probably the worst part of missing someone was never being able to tell them about things.

Dillon rested his head on his arms for a moment. Mary Jane looked up at him out of eyes growing cloudy with age. Then Dillon raised his head and picked up

the minute hand with the tweezers. As he worked, he
made a mental note to find out what kind of food to
leave for the falcon. If she healed okay, maybe she
would nest in the spring. Carefully he inserted the
minute hand in the watch. He would just have to wait
and see, come spring.